DOCTO

In her new role as Sister at St Benedict's, Gina Brent has more important issues to think about than the outrageously antagonistic behaviour of Dr Russell Steele. But when Dr Steele goes out of his way to be charming can she stop herself from loving him?

*Books you will enjoy
in our Doctor–Nurse series*

DOCTOR'S DIAGNOSIS

BY

GRACE READ

MILLS & BOON LIMITED
London · Sydney · Toronto

First published in Great Britain 1984
by Mills & Boon Limited, 15–16 Brook's Mews,
London W1A 1DR

© Grace Read 1984

Australian copyright 1984
Philippine copyright 1984

ISBN 0 263 74597 X

Set in 11 on 12 pt Linotron Times
03–0384–48,714

*Photoset by Rowland Phototypesetting Ltd
Bury St Edmunds, Suffolk
Made and printed in Great Britain by
Richard Clay (The Chaucer Press) Ltd
Bungay, Suffolk*

CHAPTER ONE

A LATE October Monday morning and on the fourth floor of St Benedict's Hospital in North London the day staff of Harvey Ward were gathered in the office to hear the report.

'Professor Phipps had a good night,' began Molly Stevens, starting with the patient in the private room.

Staff Nurse Gina Brent's blue eyes widened. 'Professor Phipps?' she queried, 'what's he doing here?'

Molly looked up from her Kardex notes. 'What? Oh, of course, you've been away, haven't you. Yes, he's been in about ten days now ... viral pneumonia.'

'Oh dear! Poor Sister Lewis. Does that mean their wedding is off?'

'I don't suppose so, although she has been in a flat spin about him, naturally. But Russell Steele is quite satisfied with his progress.'

'Russell Steele?' echoed Gina, looking even more surprised, 'who's he?'

Molly Stevens laughed. 'The latest line in registrars. Actually he was Phippsy's sidekick at the Heathside, they say. It's rumoured he'll take over here from the Prof as consultant eventually. Anyway, to get on, the Prof's temp is still fluctuating slightly but it was normal this morning. He's still rather sorry for himself. You know medics, always uptight over their own symptoms.'

'That's all I need on my first day back,' sighed Gina, 'a self-diagnostic doctor! Still, he's a darling really. Can't imagine how Andrea ever got him to the point of proposing, though.'

Third-year student Lynn Davis giggled. 'She probably proposed to him.'

Continuing with the rest of her report on Acute Medical, Molly went on: 'Mr Morris came in yesterday. Haematuria, query renal calculus. He's awaiting investigation.' Coming to the end of her comments on the remaining patients, she stretched and yawned extravagantly. 'That's about it, folks. Boy, I'm shattered. Lead me to my little bed.' And with her cloak about her shoulders, she ambled off to her well-earned rest.

With Sister Andrea Lewis being on days off, as senior staff nurse Gina found herself in charge. This morning the ward was short-staffed, one of their number being off sick.

'Start getting patients sitting out for breakfast,' Gina prompted the three students on duty with her. 'I'll see if I can get some extra help.' She picked up the telephone to contact the Nursing Officer.

The answer she received was not encouraging. 'All the wards are pretty stretched this morning, Nurse Brent. There's a lot of flu about. I'll try to get you an agency nurse, but I can't promise.'

Well, it wouldn't be the first time they'd had to manage. Putting down the phone with a sigh of resignation, Gina hurried into the ward to familiarise herself with her patients. There were many new faces since her last spell of duty a fortnight previously. She thought she had better start with Professor Phipps.

The Professor was in his early fifties, a small dynamo of a man with wild iron-grey hair and bright bird-like eyes under bushy brows. He was usually so involved with work that he overlooked unimportant details like eating. More often than not his tie was askew and he had even been known to wear odd shoes. As a diagnostician, though, he was quite brilliant. Sister Andrea Lewis, in her late thirties, had been in love with the man for some years. She was super-efficient and level-headed. Everyone agreed she would be good for the Professor; he needed someone to take care of him. Gina hoped their marriage plans would not take a setback.

'Good morning, sir,' she said, entering the Professor's room with a sympathetic smile, 'I'm very sorry to find you here.'

He paused in the act of checking his own pulse rate. 'Ah! Nurse Brent. How nice to see you, my dear.'

'How are you feeling? Did you have a good night?'

'Hardly slept at all,' he said, wheezing, his broad brow furrowed. 'My pulse is ninety, you know, and my temperature is still erratic.'

'That's only to be expected,' said Gina calmly. 'You're doing very well, I hear. Now, what do you fancy for breakfast. A little scrambled egg?'

He shuddered. 'Ugh! Can't bear the stuff. A

small portion of porridge perhaps . . .'

'All right, sir. And is it tea or coffee?'

'Gone off both, I'm afraid. My taste buds are appalling.'

Gina curbed a smile. 'You know you ought to drink as much as you can,' she reminded him. 'That's what you tell other patients, isn't it?' She poured a glass of water from the jug on his locker. 'Shall I put some cordial in this?'

He patted her hand. 'I'll just have the water. I'll be good, I promise you. You get on, my dear, I'm sure you've plenty to do.' He called her back as she was about to leave. 'What time are you expecting young Steele? I'd like a word.'

'Yes, of course. He'll be taking your outpatients' clinic this morning, I expect. But he's bound to be up after that.'

Returning to the ward Gina greeted her old patients and introduced herself to the newcomers. Meanwhile the morning work continued and when washing bowls and mouth-washes had been removed, breakfasts were served from the hot-trolley.

With everyone catered for, the staff once more assembled in the ward office. Seated at the desk, Gina assessed the work to be done, allotting special tasks to each nurse. 'Lynn, I'll do the drugs round with you this morning,' she was saying, when a sudden movement in the doorway caught her attention.

'Good morning!' said a deep, vibrant voice.

Glancing up, her eyes met those of the tall, white-coated figure standing there. That voice seemed to come from the very depths of his broad chest. There was an aura of power about his superb physique. His eyes were dark and vital, long-lashed. His hair was dark too, silky and curly, framing his angular features. She felt momentarily stunned by his presence.

'Good morning,' she returned, finding her voice at last.

'Russell Steele,' he announced. 'I'm looking in on Professor Phipps for a moment. No . . . no need to come,' he went on as she half rose to join him. With a brief impersonal smile he disappeared in the direction of the Professor's room.

'Wow!' Gina exclaimed, looking round at the doting faces of her dreamy-eyed staff, 'So *that's* Russell Steele. Someone might have warned me!'

Lynn Davis giggled. 'Bit of an improvement on Phippsy, isn't he?'

Gina raised her neat eyebrows equivocally. 'Hmmm!' she said, 'There's not much wrong with the Prof . . . all the patients like him. I'll reserve my judgment on this one until I see how the ward round goes.'

With no extra help turning up that morning the pace was hectic. There were the very sick patients to be bed-bathed, intravenous bags to be checked and changed, specimens to be collected and tested, injections to be given, and the inevitable calls for bottles and bedpans. In addition there were visits from the physiotherapists and dietician, and the path. lab. technicians collecting their blood samples for analysis. Gladys, the ward cleaner, exchanging good-humoured banter with the patients as she worked between the beds, added to the general activity.

Lunches had been served and some semblance of peace restored to the ward before Gina had an opportunity of properly studying all the case histories of the newer patients. She had scarcely got down to her reading before the medical team arrived to do the ward round. Russell Steele was accompanied by the senior houseman Peter Smythe and three medical students.

Peter grinned as Gina came out to greet them. Her creamy cheeks were pink with exertion and with her russet curls escaping from the diminutive frilled cap, she presented a deceptively fragile appearance. 'Hi!' he said, 'Back, are you? Have you met Dr Steele? He's standing in for Professor Phipps.'

Dr Steele inclined his well-groomed head in her direction and gave her his brief, remote smile. 'Right. Where shall we start?'

'Will you see the Professor first?' Gina suggested.

He considered for a moment. 'No . . . I'll deal with the ward, and then I needn't hold up the rest of you while I see the Professor.'

The nurses scurried around, whipping up empty lunch dishes as Peter Smythe led the way to the first patient. Gina pushed out the notes' trolley and hurried after the doctors. She grabbed Sharon Evans, a rather untidy first-year student, to take charge of the trolley while she herself stood ready to give the doctors any assistance needed.

The group made its leisurely progress around the ward, pausing to examine charts and discuss developments. Gina drew the bed curtains, removed dressings, gave information and prepared patients for their chests to be sounded or other parts to be examined.

They came to the latest admission—Mr Morris, the middle-aged man who had come in the previous day with an acute kidney infection.

'May I have the notes, please?' asked Dr Steele. He approached the patient with a pleasant greeting.

'Mr Morris's folder, Sharon,' murmured Gina.

The junior riffled through the folders and extracted a thick wad of papers, passing them to Gina who put them into the registrar's outstretched hand.

Dr Steele, studying the most recent information, frowned. 'Have there been any investigations?' he asked Peter Smythe. 'I don't see any reports.'

'We sent off a sterile urine specimen but we haven't had the results yet.'

'I see. What about these blackouts?' the registrar asked the patient with an enquiring smile.

Mr Morris looked puzzled. 'I don't have blackouts, Doctor,' he said.

Dr Steele referred to the notes again. 'Well, try to remember the last time that you did have a blackout.'

'But I've never had a blackout in my life,' the patient insisted, 'only backache and this pain on passing water.'

The registrar's dark brows contracted. He

referred to the name on the folder. 'I suppose you *are* George Morris?'

'No . . . my name's Stephen.'

Closing the folder Russell Steele handed it back to Gina with exaggerated patience. 'May I have the right notes, please?' The tone of voice was mild enough, but his look spoke volumes.

'Sorry!' she said, feeling her colour rise. Searching for the correct notes herself, she handed them to him.

'Thank you. That's better. Well, Mr *Stephen* Morris,' he went on with a slight smile, 'we need some more information here. We'll get an intravenous pyelogram done . . . that's just our name for a special X-ray process,' he explained as Mr Morris looked apprehensive. 'They'll run a special dye into your kidneys to pinpoint the trouble. If it's gravel we may be able to disperse it. If it's a stone I'll have to refer you to a surgeon. But let's wait and see, shall we?' He patted the patient's hand before moving on to the next bed.

The rest of the round proceeded satisfactorily with Gina double-checking to make sure that there were no more mix-ups with papers. Sharon Evans had been on the ward for two months and she should have known the patients, but she was slaphappy sometimes and always inclined to get flustered in the presence of doctors. Making allowances, Gina conceded that two patients with the same surname was rather confusing. This time there had been no harm done. All the same, she wished it hadn't happened on her first contact with the new registrar.

At the conclusion of his round Dr Steele thanked the team and left them to carry out the tests he had ordered. 'I'll see the Professor now,' he said to Gina. She followed him to the private room but outside the door he paused and looked at her with a glint of mockery in his dark eyes. 'I don't think I'm likely to confuse this patient with anyone else, Nurse Brent. I'll let you know if I need you.'

Gina wrinkled her small nose behind him as he went in and closed the door, but she couldn't help a wry smile. Although tolerance did not appear to be one of his virtues, there was obviously a sense of humour lurking somewhere behind that quelling manner.

Maybe Russell Steele had arrived too quickly, Gina reflected as she went back to her work. He didn't look very old despite the odd silver hair in the dark waves around his temples. Mid-thirties perhaps? At that age he must be pretty brilliant to be fit to step into the Professor's shoes. And with those looks he'd only have to lift a finger to have all the staff and patients drooling over him. Well, here was one person who was not going to join his admiration society. She had met his sort before. Probably thought he came with a personal recommendation from God, Gina mused. Underneath, though, he was only a man; he'd have his hang-ups like most people.

The second shift had by now come on duty and things were a little less frantic. The first shift went to lunch and Gina handed over to Staff Nurse Zoe Wynford before taking her own lunch break. As she was about to leave the Professor's bell rang. 'I'll answer that before I go,' she told Zoe.

In the private room she found Dr Steele putting his stethoscope back into his coat pocket while the Professor fumbled with the buttons on his pyjama jacket.

'Be a dear girl and fix my pillows, will you?' Professor Phipps appealed to Gina. 'This feller's been pulling me about.'

'Of course, sir.' She smiled and helped him forward. Plumping up the pillows, she arranged them to his satisfaction.

'That's better, my dear.' He settled back comfortably. 'They've a special knack, these nurses, eh Russell?'

'I imagine so, although fortunately I haven't been on the receiving end so far,' said Dr Steele with lazy irony, casting a critical glance her way.

Embarrassed to find herself the focus of attention Gina made great play of straightening the sheet.

The registrar transferred his gaze back to his patient. 'You're doing splendidly . . . temperature coming down nicely,' he observed.

Professor Phipps grunted and held Gina's hand. 'These pretty young things are enough to send anyone's temperature rocketing.'

'Even so, I expect we'll get you to the church on time.'

'Providing I don't develop a pleural effusion . . . or even cardiac failure, the way that physio pummels me,' said the Professor dolefully.

Russell Steele chuckled. It was a deep-throated

infectious sound which had an odd effect on Gina's determination to resist his undeniable personal attraction. 'I shall hold Nurse Brent responsible if you do,' he said with a twisted smile. 'Don't exhaust yourself with too much talking. Let's see . . . you'll be off the Ampicillin in a couple of days.' He studied the Professor's medication sheet. 'You should be getting your appetite back after that. I'll be in to see you again tomorrow, sir.'

The Professor gazed after his protégé as he left the room. 'Fine chap. He'll go to the top.'

'Yes,' agreed Gina dutifully, tidying the locker top. 'Will Sister Lewis be coming in today?'

'I hope so . . . unless she wants me to die of boredom. This enforced idleness makes me feel like a parasite.'

She laughed. 'That you certainly are not. Make the most of the rest while you can.'

Going off to her own belated lunch, Gina met up with her flatmate Esther in the staff canteen. They had not seen each other since Gina's return from holiday, Esther having spent the night at her parents' home in the neighbouring town. They had a great deal of news to catch up on, especially the furore caused by the Professor's illness.

'Sister Lewis was in a right state at first,' said Esther, sipping her coffee. 'I mean, all the wedding arrangements made etcetera . . . will they still be able to go through with it?'

Gina took a mouthful of cottage pie which had been the only choice left on the rather limited canteen menu. 'Russell Steele seems to think he'll be able to make it.'

'Oh! So you've met him, have you? Tasty, isn't he?' Esther grinned. 'Even Sister Trant is impressed . . . and her married with two kids.'

'Hmm . . . a bit full of himself, I thought,' returned Gina. 'Maybe because I got off on the wrong foot with him.' She related the incident of the mix-up in case notes. 'I should have remembered Sharon Evans always goes to pieces in the presence of supermen. My fault for not checking. He withered me with a glance,' she added. 'He has a nice turn in sarcasm.'

'The dominant male!' intoned Esther dramatically. 'That's part of his charm.'

'Oh, come on! What happened to the advocate of women's lib?'

Esther curbed a smile and sighed. 'It's an uphill battle when sex rears its ugly head. I was reading one of our patient's magazines, and it said that the average male thinks about sex six times in every hour. How can you fight that?'

'I shouldn't think Russell Steele even needs to think about it,' said Gina with a giggle. 'Probably gets it handed to him on a plate.'

They went on to discuss more immediate matters. 'Do we need any shopping?' Esther asked.

'Yes, bread, tea and toilet rolls. I'll pick them up on my way home.'

Returning to the ward, Gina bumped into Sister Lewis emerging from the Professor's room. 'Hallo! Have a good holiday?' she asked, sounding quite cheerful.

'Yes, thanks. I was only staying with my married sister down in Lyndhurst. Still, it's nice there, with the New Forest. Andrea . . . I'm so sorry about the Professor,' she sympathised. 'I hope it won't mess up your plans.'

'Oh well, it's just one of those things,' said Andrea. 'We've still got three weeks to go and he's doing okay, isn't he? Good thing it happened now and not later.'

'Yes . . . and he's been pretty fit up till now . . . doesn't drink or smoke. We'll probably have him up tomorrow. He could be out by the weekend. That still gives you a fortnight to get him on his feet. Have you got a honeymoon planned?'

'Oh, haven't I told you? Perry's got a lecture tour fixed up in the States . . . we're going to combine the two, so we'll be away for about three months. Russell will carry on here for Perry, but it's my guess he'll take over permanently before long. I've given in my notice, by the way. You'll apply for the job, won't you?'

'Me?' Gina hesitated. 'Do you think I should?'

'Why not? You've done all the right courses and you've been staffing here for a year. I think you'd be ideal. I'll give you a good write-up.'

Having been away Gina had presumed that applications might have gone in in her absence. Obviously a decision had not yet been made or Sister Lewis would have known. She did feel capable of handling the job; she already did when Andrea Lewis was off-duty. Anyway, there was certainly no harm in trying.

She was still mulling it over with a degree of eager anticipation as she drove home in her Fiat that evening, stopping off first at the supermarket

to pick up the provisions. It was the height of the
rush hour when she again joined the traffic in the
High Street to resume her journey. With pedes-
trians constantly pressing buttons at crossing points
and traffic lights changing at intersections it was
stop-go all the way, and she made slow progress.

Gina slipped into a space in the nearside lane,
braked for the umpteenth time and waited patiently for the traffic to move. Wrapped in thought, she
absently noted the dark green Jaguar which drew
up alongside her. Her glance wandered idly to the
girl in the passenger seat, long ash-blonde hair in
stylish disorder. Then, with a start of recognition,
she caught sight of the man behind the wheel. It was
Russell Steele.

Quickly Gina turned her head in case he should
notice her . . . and found herself gazing into the
round face of a police officer tapping on her window. He was a very young policeman. Anxiously
she wound down the window. 'Is anything wrong?'

'Are you aware that you're travelling in a bus
lane, miss?' he demanded accusingly.

'Oh! Sorry.' With a bit of rapid thinking she
found an excuse. 'I wanted to turn left at the next
junction.'

'Then why aren't you indicating?'

Looking suitably contrite, she remedied the
omission. The lights changed and he motioned her
on. She hadn't really wanted to turn left but since
she was now indicating and in case he was still
looking, she thought she had better do so. It took
her right out of her way.

'You've been a long time,' Esther said when

Gina at last staggered in with the shopping. 'Did you get everything?'

'Yes . . . and a ticking off by a bossy copper into the bargain.' She dumped the shopping on the kitchen table and detailed the events of her journey home. 'Men! I bet he wasn't a day over twenty. A bit of power goes to their heads. Bus lanes were the last thing on my mind,' she went on ruefully, 'all I was thinking about was applying for the sister's job. Hope to goodness Steele didn't spot me or he'll think I'm completely feather-brained.'

'He was with a girl?' Esther queried. 'Wife or girlfriend would you say?'

'How should I know? But he doesn't wear a wedding ring, does he,' Gina added, remembering the strong capable hands she had watched examining patients, 'although he does have a signet ring on his little finger.'

CHAPTER TWO

IN SPITE of his own misgivings, and to the relief of Andrea Lewis, Professor Phipps made a good recovery. The following Monday he was collected by his married sister who, much to his disgust, insisted on whisking him away to convalesce at her Wimbledon home for a few days.

'Thank God for antibiotics,' sighed Andrea, returning to the sideward to deal with the remainder of his belongings after seeing the great man on his way.

Clearing out the locker while Lynn Davis disinfected the bed, Gina agreed. 'Yes,' she said, 'pneumonia isn't the scourge it used to be.' She went on to ask about the wedding plans. 'Are you going ahead as arranged?'

'Oh, yes. The banns have been called once already,' Andrea told her. The ceremony was to take place at St Benedict's, the picturesque old church from which the hospital derived its name, and many distinguished members of the profession would be amongst the guests. 'Sorry we can't invite you all to the reception, but there'll be a staff party sometime in the residents' dining room.'

'What are you wearing?' Gina wanted to know.

'I've bought a brown velvet suit, braided, and there's a frilly cream silk blouse to go under it.'

'Sounds lovely. We are going to miss you, though.'

'Me too,' said Andrea with a reflective smile. 'I'm rather fond of this old place. After all, I'm almost part of the furniture, but looking after Perry is going to be a full time job . . .' She paused as she picked up a pot of pink cyclamen from the window-sill. 'He won't want this . . . put it in the ward for me, will you?'

Gina carried the plant through and placed it on the centre table, stopping to answer the telephone on her way back. 'A & E just rang,' she reported to Andrea, 'they'll be sending us a sixteen-year-old diabetic for stabilising. He came in with a hypo.' She glanced at her watch. 'It's almost time for my interview now . . . may I go?'

'Yes, you push off, love, and good luck.'

In the staff room Gina put on a clean apron over her lavender-striped uniform dress, tidied her hair and rearranged her cap before taking the lift down to Administration. Some days previously she had filled in the comprehensive application form for the Sister's post on Harvey Ward. Now she found herself sitting outside the office in the company of three other hopefuls, all in mufti and none of whom she knew.

After exchanging brief smiles with the other candidates she tried to concentrate her mind on the correct answers to questions that were likely to be asked. But her brain felt woolly. Oh, what the hell, she decided, once she got inside things would prob-ably come back to her; and either she measured up to requirements or she didn't. Anyway, she still had plenty of years ahead of her. If this interview didn't come off at least it would be good experience for the future.

The door of the office opened and Miss Chard, the Senior Nursing Officer, looked out. 'Nurse Brent, will you come in now?' she asked pleasantly.

Mentally squaring her shoulders, Gina rose and took a deep breath before entering, not knowing exactly how many people she would be facing. She found a selection panel of three. Seated at the desk alongside Miss Chard was the familiar figure of the Nursing Officer for the Medical Unit, who was a fair-minded person. But her heart skipped a beat at the sight of the third member of the panel. It was Russell Steele. He sat lounging in an easy chair to one side of the desk, looking her over with apparent indifference and not giving the least sign of recognition.

'Sit down, Nurse Brent,' Miss Chard invited, indicating the chair opposite the desk.

With her stomach in knots, Gina sat. Clasping her hands in her lap she waited for the inquisition to begin. Three pairs of critical eyes focused upon her. She knew that the Nursing Officers, having followed her progress through the hospital, might be halfway to wanting her to be acceptable. All else being equal, internal applicants were often favoured over outsiders. But when it came to the Senior Medical Registrar, she was not at all certain of how he would feel.

Contrary to her expectations the interview proved to be more in the nature of a friendly chat than the grilling she had anticipated. When her hospital record had been summed up, she was asked a number of questions on ward management and her attitude to the handling of student training. Answering up, Gina's nervousness vanished as she gave her views frankly and confidently.

Instinctively she avoided looking in Russell Steele's direction, but nonetheless she was very conscious of his watchful gaze upon her. At first he seemed content to let the others have their say, but later he put his own questions on certain matters so that she had no option but to face him. Her answers concerning the care of various diseases seemed to satisfy him. Finally he put to her:

'And suppose you disagreed with a doctor's proposed course of treatment, would you carry out his instructions without question?'

That was tricky. He sat with eyes narrowed, observing her closely, one leg nonchalantly propped on the other knee. Absently she noted the sinewy strength of his thigh muscles beneath the well-tailored grey trousers. She hesitated, then met his gaze boldly. 'If I felt it was not in the patient's best interest,' she said, 'I should certainly make my views known.'

A small silence followed. 'Thank you, Nurse. That's all I need to know,' said Russell Steele.

She thought she must have blown it. She looked towards the Nursing Officers but they were busy writing. Miss Chard gave her a brief nod of dismissal. 'Thank you, Nurse. We'll let you know when we've seen the other applicants.'

'Well, how did it go?' Sister Lewis asked when Gina returned to the ward.

'Hard to tell,' she shrugged. 'They've got these other people to see first. Miss Chard said she'd let me know.'

The arrival of their new patient from A & E put an end to personal matters. The Casualty nurse handed in the case notes and Gina went out to welcome the newcomer.

'Hallo! We know you, don't we?' she said, recognising the freckle-faced lad. 'It's Ben. You were in with a hypo back in the summer, weren't you?'

Young Ben grinned a little sheepishly. 'Yeah!'

Accompanying him, his mother sighed. 'And he's going to miss his exams again, like he did in the summer.'

Gina shook her head despairingly. 'What are we going to do with him? Perhaps he won't need to be in too long.' She directed the porter to wheel him to the vacant bed and after settling him in, she went off to make out the necessary charts.

The next couple of hours were full of activity. There was Mr Stephen Morris to be prepared to go down for his pyelogram and Mr George Morris to be given his pre-med and made ready for the gastroscopy theatre. Thoughts of her interview for the Sister's post faded into the background until the telephone call which came at four o'clock.

She was writing up her Kardex before going off-duty when Andrea said: 'They're asking for you down in Admin. Don't you dare go off without letting me know what happens.'

Hurrying to the staff room, Gina tidied up again before taking the lift to the ground floor. None of the other applicants was in the waiting area. She didn't know whether that was good or bad as she knocked on the office door.

'Come in,' called Miss Chard.

Prepared for anything, Gina entered. She found the Senior Nursing Officer alone.

'Well, Nurse Brent,' Miss Chard said briskly, 'we've decided to offer you the job. We all thought you were the most suitable applicant.'

'Oh! Thank you.' Gina coloured with delight.

'Sit down, my dear.' Miss Chard motioned her to a chair and proceeded to discuss the details of her contract, including the amount by which her salary would increase in line with the extra responsibility involved. She was to have a fresh medical to ensure her fitness and there would be the new uniform to be measured for.

Racing back to the ward with her good news, she was embarrassed to find Russell Steele in the office writing up his notes after visiting the new diabetic patient.

'Dr Steele has told me,' Andrea said, smiling broadly, 'but I didn't think you had much to worry about.'

'And I trust we shan't disagree on *too* many points,' Steele commented drily as he finished his writing and returned his ballpoint to his pocket.

'Oh, you'll find Gina has a good grasp of everything required of her on the ward,' Sister Lewis assured him.

'Hmmm! Maybe a little brushing up on her Highway Code would be useful in other areas.' With a cryptic smile he went on his way.

Andrea looked puzzled. 'What's he on about?'

'Clever clogs!' Gina muttered, gritting her teeth and controlling the urge to explode, 'I got into a bus lane by mistake one day last week. *He* happened to draw up alongside me when the police pounced.'

'Oh! Is that all? Well, men behind the wheel are totally irrational. They think everyone else on the road is a fool. You'll have to allow him that little dig . . . expect he couldn't resist it.'

'And I suppose he did vote in my favour,' Gina allowed, too thrilled to let his sarcasm worry her unduly. Gathering her things together and putting on her cloak, she made her way down to the ground floor and along a corridor towards the main entrance.

'Excuse me!' A young woman approached her diffidently. 'Could you tell me where I have to go with this?'

Gina studied the scrawled address on the envelope held out to her. 'Oh, you want Obstetrics. That's in the new wing at the back. Turn right at the bottom of this corridor and go under the arch,' she pointed. 'You'll find the building on your left.'

Although the hospital was well signposted it could be a complicated maze to strangers. She remembered how lost she had felt when she had arrived as a student, over five years ago now. It had taken her quite a while to familiarise herself with the many departments. And since her arrival there had been a number of alterations and additions as funds allowed. The main reception area was almost like a miniature village these days with its coffee bar, bookshop, florist's, even a bank.

Continuing on her way down the corridor, she

saw Peter Smythe pinning something on the green baize notice board and stopped to tell him of her new appointment.

'Congratulations!' he said heartily. 'Tuppence to speak to you now, I suppose.'

She laughed. 'I thought I'd had it. Steele asked me if I'd question treatment I disagreed with . . . and I stuck my neck out and said that I would.'

'Good for you. You've a right to your views . . . and even the experts can be fallible.' He pointed to the notice he had just pinned to the board. 'You joining us again this year?'

'What's that?' Gina peered at the announcement scrawled with a red felt-tipped pen. It requested all staff interested in taking part in the annual carol concert at the Royal Festival Hall to attend for the preliminary practice in St Benedict's Parish Hall on the forthcoming Wednesday. 'Oh, that seems to have come round quickly again,' she said. 'Yes, I wouldn't miss it. See you there.'

She went on her way even more buoyed up at the prospect of once more taking part in the London hospitals combined choirs event, the proceeds of which went to a cancer fund. Both she and Esther had joined in the previous year. They had averagely tuneful voices and found it an uplifting experience, joining with hundreds of other nurses and doctors in this joyful prelude to Christmas. She remembered the triumphal sound of the fanfare of trumpeters, and the stirring music of the military band, and the humour of the professional conductor who had put them all through their paces.

Driving home, Gina had only one regret. This

time there would be no member of her family amongst the vast audience. Last year her mother and father had been there, together with her sister and brother-in-law, and they had all gone out to dinner afterwards. Now there was a breach between her mother and father, after twenty-five years of marriage. Her mother had gone off to Australia on the pretext of visiting her sister, and her father was on a tour of the Far East for his shipping company. Gina's sister Melanie was expecting a baby mid-December, so that would put paid to support from that direction. A pity, since this time she would be wearing a dark blue uniform and the frilled cap of her new Sister's status.

But at least her promotion would please her father. He had always been ambitious for his two girls and he had not been entirely in favour of Gina's choice of career; he would be glad to know she was making a success of it. Melanie had disappointed him when she had dropped out of University at twenty-one to marry John, a school teacher.

Arriving back at the flat, Gina remembered that Esther was on a late. It was disappointing not to be able to share her good news immediately. But another car on the paved forecourt in front of the house told her that one of the boys in the upstairs flat was already home.

The girls occupied the bottom half of a Victorian house in Golders Green. The upper half was shared by dental student Mark and his friend Jason, a trainee chef at a London hotel. In the main hall there was a door shutting off the staircase to the upper rooms, but it was never closed and the four of them lived more like brothers and sisters. The girls were useful with needles and cotton and the boys were handy with screwdrivers and so forth. Their love-lives were a thing apart, but it was always handy to have a partner available if needed.

Minutes after Gina had let herself into the house Mark came skimming down the stairs. 'Hi, kid! Got any coffee? We're clean out.'

'Yes, help yourself . . . and make me some, will you? Although I should be celebrating with something stronger,' she flung over her shoulder as she disappeared into her bedroom.

Mark busied himself in the kitchen. She heard him clattering about and whistling cheerfully while she took off her uniform and wriggled into jeans and a sweater.

'What was that about celebrating?' he wanted to know, bringing in two steaming mugs and flopping on the side of her bed.

She took the coffee and sat on a fat cushion on the floor. 'I'm going up in the world,' she said. 'It's Sister Brent now . . . or will be when Andrea Lewis marries her professor.'

'Great!' Mark exclaimed, ruffling her bright locks. 'You'll be hob-nobbing with the top brass now, I suppose. When are you moving out?'

'Oh, don't be daft. It will mean some extra cash in the bank though . . . which can't be bad considering you lot are always skint.'

'Well, I've only got another year of being an impoverished student . . . provided I get my finals, that is.'

'You will,' said Gina, feeling optimistic for them all. 'Then perhaps I'll even let you have a go at my pearlies.'

Mark set his mug down and slithered to the floor, squatting in front of her. 'You've got very nice pearlies.' He took her chin in his hand. 'Open up and let me see your fillings?'

She did as he ordered and he peered into her mouth, looking this way and that. 'Mmmm . . . not bad, not bad.' Suddenly, taking her unawares, he clamped his mouth over hers.

Wriggling free, she giggled. 'Cut it out, Mark.'

He smoothed back a sandy forelock and looked at her impishly. 'I fancy you something rotten, if you must know.'

'No, you don't. It's just your libido acting up because I'm available and there's nobody else at the moment. The next bit of stuff behind the bar and I'd be "good old Gina" again.'

'You mean I don't turn you on?' he said mournfully.

'Fortunately, no. That *would* put a spanner in the works. Go and take a cold shower or something. If you're still available I'll let you take me to the Nurses' Ball next month.'

'Right, lover, you're on,' he said cheerfully.

Jason arrived home then, and he too was on top of the world. That weekend he was to go off to Paris until Christmas, on a student exchange basis. 'The guy who was going has caught measles and I've got to take his place. Shame, isn't it?' and he whooped with laughter.

After some mutual back-slapping the boys took

themselves off to their own quarters, leaving Gina thoughtful. She hoped there was no hint of truth behind Mark's play-acting. She was fond of him, but only as a friend, and with Jason away he was liable to seek their company more than usual. She wished he would find himself a steady girlfriend.

Shelving the problem for the moment, she decided to ring her sister at Lyndhurst.

'Hi, Gina!' Melanie exclaimed. 'We've been trying to reach you all day,' she rattled on without pausing for breath. 'There's someone here to speak to you . . . I'll pass you over.'

'Hallo, darling!' came a familiar voice.

For a moment Gina could hardly believe her ears, then she squealed, 'Mum! When did you get back?'

Her mother laughed softly. 'I made up my mind on the spur of the moment. I couldn't think of letting my first grandchild arrive and me not here.'

'You should have let me know . . . I could have met you at Heathrow perhaps.'

'Well, I didn't get in until nine o'clock last night, and I didn't know what your duties were, so I thought it better to come straight on here. Can you get some time off?'

'Oh dear, I've used up all my holiday, worse luck,' said Gina, 'and there's such a lot on between now and Christmas . . . I'll have to see what I can do.'

'I'll be coming up to town myself anyway,' her mother put in. 'I want to do some Christmas shopping . . . and there are some of my things at the Kensington flat I need to collect.'

'Dad's still away, isn't he? What are you going to do when he gets back?'

Her mother demurred. 'It depends . . . we'll have to wait and see.'

Gina sighed. When you loved both your parents it was hard to see the rift widening between them. Although it had not been openly talked about she knew there had been another woman in it somewhere. It was asking a lot for her mother to forgive and forget.

'And how are things with you?' Laura Brent enquired, reminding Gina of the reason for her phone call.

'Couldn't be better,' she returned brightly. 'You're going to have a Sister for a daughter. How's that?'

'You've got promotion? That's wonderful, darling. You must have inherited your father's brains. You've got more drive than your unaspiring old mum.'

'Don't be so modest,' Gina laughed. 'All my better instincts come from you . . . including my stubborn streak. And there's more to life than getting on.'

They had a long talk, catching up on recent events. 'And I'll definitely come to the carol concert,' her mother promised, 'provided the baby doesn't decide to arrive on that particular day, of course.'

When Esther arrived home she had already heard of Gina's success. 'So you couldn't have gone down too badly with Russell Steele,' she observed, stripping off her uniform and getting into her dressing-gown while her friend set about getting something to eat for both of them.

In the kitchen Gina made a doubtful face as she opened a can of oxtail soup and put it on the gas stove to heat. 'Being new, he probably thought he'd better keep in with the SNOs,' she said derisively when Esther joined her.

'Rubbish! With every female in the place hearing heavenly music if he so much as smiles at them? He hardly needs to "keep in" does he?'

Gina stirred the soup and rescued some toast from under the grill. 'Funny,' she smiled, 'I must be tone-deaf then, because he doesn't get through to me.' But even as she spoke, the memory of his dark eyes coolly appraising her sent a disturbing tingle down her spine.

At the Wednesday carol practice in the church hall St Benedict's were joined by groups from two other hospitals.

'Look who's here!' nudged Esther as she and Gina joined the lively crowd which had gathered.

Gina had needed no alerting. She had been aware of Russell Steele's dominant presence as soon as she entered the hall. He was not the kind of man you could overlook. 'Peter must have talked him into it,' she said, her eyes on his shapely head set square on those broad shoulders. He unexpectedly glanced her way and she quickly averted her gaze, disconcerted to have been caught staring.

'Will you sort yourselves out into groups?' said Peter Smythe, calling them all to attention. 'We'll have the sopranos over here, contraltos over there, and baritones here.' He distributed the musical parts and seated himself at the ancient upright piano to try out the programme.

They tackled some of the old traditional carols with descants and counter-melodies, going on to some lesser-known but attractive Christmas songs from other countries.

'Right. We'll have "Ring out, wild bells",' said Peter, 'and then call it a day before the pubs close.'

The words of Tennyson, set to rousing music, were always guaranteed to bring a lump to Gina's throat . . .

> Ring in the valiant man and free,
> The larger heart, the kindlier hand,
> Ring out the darkness of the land,
> Ring in the Christ that is to be.

It seemed to epitomise all that one hoped for at the beginning of a new year, all those good resolutions which so often petered out.

The practice concluded, most of the singers made a beeline to moisten their throats at the local Fox & Grapes, mainly separating into their respective hospital groups.

Peter Smythe and Paul Waring, the surgical registrar, took it upon themselves to buy the first round for the St Benedict's crowd and went off towards the bar. Gina and Esther stood chatting with Sister Sally Yates from Theatre until the boys came back with their drinks.

'That went really well, I thought,' said Peter, looking pleased with himself. 'We're stronger on baritones this year with Russell joining us. He used to be with a singing group in his Cambridge days, so he was telling me.'

They all glanced towards the bar where Russell was talking with a former colleague from the Heathside.

'The good fairy must have been working over-time at his christening,' said Sally. 'Brawn, brains and a baritone into the bargain.'

'Hm! Pity she missed out on the brotherly love,' murmured Gina.

Peter chuckled. 'Now, now! Just because he caught you out the other day. I know it wasn't your fault, but when you're in charge you have to take the blame. Wait till you get into your blue job . . . she'll know all about carrying the can then, won't she, Sally?'

'Oh, yes. Uneasy lies the head with extra frills to its cap,' cracked Sally.

The subject of their discussion sauntered over to join them. Drawing him into the conversation, Peter said: 'We're just warning Gina that she'll have to develop a thick skin on her way up the ladder. Power has its price, eh?'

Russell Steele let his inscrutable brown eyes take a leisurely tour of Gina, from the burnished titian curls framing her piquant face, to the swell of her small breasts beneath the roomy blue sweater and the neat hips encased in navy corduroy jeans. He took a long drink of his beer before replying: 'I'm sure she'll rise to the challenge.'

'There's confidence for you,' said Peter, putting an arm around her shoulders.

She widened her blue eyes. 'Is that what it was? I thought it might be sarcasm,' she returned sweetly.

Russell momentarily lost his detachment. His eyes glinted. 'You're nothing if not direct, are you?'

Tactfully Esther took the heat out of the situation. 'I could do with a refill,' she said, and the repartee took on a lighter note.

All the same, Gina was not comfortable in Russell Steele's presence. She felt herself under observation; not as a person, more as a piece of equipment to be assessed. It was a relief when it was closing time and they went their separate ways.

But even though he was out of sight it was not so easy to banish him from her mind. His manner annoyed her. She might have been an inanimate object he was casting his eye over. Well, she was a person as well as a nurse, and she was not going to be patronised by any toffee-nosed registrar who thought he had only to crook his little finger to have everyone jumping.

'How is he with your patients, Esther?' Gina asked curiously as they drove home.

'Russell Steele, you mean?' Esther was on a female medical ward. 'They all seem to like him.'

'And with the staff?'

'Pleasant, but professional, *you* know.'

'Acts like the lord of the manor, you mean?'

Esther laughed. 'Well, you'd expect him to be a bit on his dignity, wouldn't you? Makes him all the more interesting really. Why?'

'It gets under my skin to be treated as if I didn't

exist,' Gina protested. She parked the car on the paved court in front of the flat. 'I think I shall treat *him* like he's got the plague. Let him take the stuffing out of that.'

'Well! I've never known you to get so steamed up over a guy before. *I'm* supposed to be the touchy one.'

'Mutual antipathy, I expect. You can't like everyone.'

'He's going to be around a long time,' Esther warned. 'Someone's going to have to climb down . . . and I can't see it being him.'

CHAPTER THREE

IT WAS foggy when Gina set off for early duty the following morning. Pavements and fences dripped with moisture; cobwebs sagged damply on garden hedges and leaves lay thick and wet on the ground. Wiping the moisture from her windscreen, she reflected it was the kind of weather likely to bring bronchial sufferers to Harvey Ward. But during the morning the only new patient they admitted was a middle-aged man with congestive cardiac failure and a deep-vein thrombosis of the left leg.

Mr Trilby was on the heavy side, very febrile and distressed, with an unhealthy flush on his face. Sister Lewis and Gina made him as comfortable as they could, propping him up with pillows and putting a cradle over his legs, turning back the covers so that a watch would be kept on the affected one. His foot looked very blue.

'Can you feel your toes?' asked Andrea, touching them.

He shook his head wearily. 'No, they're sort of numb.'

Gina checked his pulse. He was already on a Heparin drip to prevent further clotting, also a heart stimulant.

He reminded her vaguely of her father. He had the same squarish build and a similar craggy face with crinkly iron-grey hair receding at the temples.

But this man was overweight and weak whereas her father was strong and vigorous.

When they had settled him down his wife came to sit with him for a while, a small worried little woman, trying to be cheerful. With Sister Lewis having gone off for her half-day, Mrs Trilby approached Gina in the office before leaving.

'How do you think he is, Nurse?' she enquired anxiously.

'We-ell, it'll take a little while for the drugs to have effect,' said Gina with caution, 'but we'll hope for the best. Doctor will be up to see him later, and then perhaps we'll be able to tell you more.' She was not at all happy about the look of that foot but she didn't want to be an alarmist.

Mr Trilby was under Russell Steele's care and he arrived during the afternoon to check on his patient. He examined the leg but made no comment. The foot was now an ominous navy-blue. Back in the office alone with Gina, he sat at the desk studying the case notes, propping his chin on his hands. 'It's no use,' he said abruptly. 'It'll have to come off. I'll arrange for the surgeon to see him.'

Gina had guessed as much, but to have her fears confirmed was still distressing. 'Poor guy,' she said.

Russell Steele shrugged his broad shoulders and passed a hand over his face. 'No option, I'm afraid. We'd better prepare him for the worst. Come on, let's get it over.'

Reluctantly she followed him back to Mr Trilby's bed, drawing the curtains to shut out the gaze of the curious.

'Mr Trilby . . . we haven't been successful in

restoring the circulation to your leg,' the doctor said, coming straight to the point. 'Your foot is gangrenous . . . it can't be saved. I'm sorry.'

Gina took hold of the patient's hand as he stared at the physician, eyes stark with panic. 'D-do you mean . . . what I think you mean?'

Russell Steele nodded. 'We have no alternative but to take it off.'

'I'm not agreeing to that!' flashed Mr Trilby angrily.

'Unfortunately, sir, it's your leg or your life.'

The patient bit trembling lips. 'L-let me think about it,' he mumbled.

'I'll get the surgeon to come and talk to you,' Russell said quietly. 'They'll be able to fit you with an artificial limb at the moment, but it might not be possible if you delay.'

'Douglas Bader had two artificial limbs and he managed fine, Mr Trilby,' Gina pointed out gently. 'It won't be so bad.'

She left the curtains partially drawn around his bed to give him time to come to terms with his situation.

In the office Russell again seated himself at the desk and phoned through to make the necessary arrangements. Gina felt angry and frustrated that their efforts had not been in time to avert the tragedy. She had to give vent to her feelings and she turned on Russell when he came off the phone.

'Did you have to be quite so brutally frank with him? You might have wrapped it up a bit.'

His own self-control slipped for a second. He flared back: 'Do you think I enjoy breaking bad news? It's his body . . . he had to face up to it sooner or later. Anyway, he has a right to honesty. People are always saying doctors never tell them anything.'

In her deeper levels of consciousness she knew that he'd had no choice, that he probably felt as bad about it as she did.

'I'll see his wife when she comes,' he added, his dark eyes hostile. 'Meanwhile perhaps you can dispense some soothing syrup.' Glowering, he pushed roughly past her and strode away.

She sensed the enormous responsibility he shouldered and the courage it took to be strong and objective when pity tugged at your heartstrings. It brought home the fact that when she officially assumed the role of Sister she was going to have to toughen up—or go under. It was impossible to carry everyone's burden for them. But Mr Trilby's fate continued to haunt her for the rest of the afternoon.

Just before going off duty Gina was in the sluice when Sharon Evans arrived with a urinal, rolling her eyes in annoyance. 'That new patient . . . he's just spilt the bottle in the bed.'

'Mr Trilby? You didn't moan at him, I hope,' said Gina quickly.

'We-ell, not exactly . . .' The junior looked a little guilty.

'Oh dear . . . he's very poorly, you know.' Gina washed and dried her hands. 'Bring a clean sheet,' she said briskly, 'and we'll change the bed for him.'

'Sorry about that,' mumbled the patient as they made him clean and comfortable again, and Gina had to smile to herself when Sharon answered up brightly:

'Not to worry . . . it happens all the time, doesn't it, Staff?'

A watery sun had broken through for a short while at midday but by four-thirty the fog had come down again in earnest. Before leaving the hospital Gina had first of all to visit the Sewing Room to be fitted for her new uniforms. Afterwards, making her way to the car park, she found the outside world shrouded in a grey blanket with lights from the surrounding buildings scarcely visible.

Searching out her car, she manoeuvred cautiously out of the hospital grounds, the fog swirling in the beam of her headlights. Sounds in the High Street were muted and traffic crawled at snail's pace. The buses seemed to have stopped running altogether. Somewhere a police siren wailed. It was eerie and frightening. Traffic lights seemed to come at her without warning. And suddenly she had no idea whereabouts she was heading. But she had to keep going. If she pulled up something might run into the back of her. All she could do was to follow the rear-lights of the car in front. Her eyes smarted as she strained to peer ahead.

She seemed to have been travelling much further than usual, but that was probably because everything was moving so slowly, Gina reflected. Presently the car ahead took a right turn. She followed it; they were going uphill and their own flat was on a rise, so she must be going in the right direction. Changing gear she continued to keep those rear-lights in view. Her leader took another right turn and presently pulled up.

Hurriedly Gina applied her own brakes. When the car in front showed no sign of moving she wound down her window and called: 'Excuse me!'

The door of the vehicle had opened and a large figure emerged backwards, lifting out a brief-case. The man appeared not to have heard her, so she pipped her horn and risked getting out herself. Gravel crunched beneath her feet; there were the dark shapes of bushes all around and, to her left, what appeared to be a large house from which a faint gleam of light filtered.

The man straightened up and turned in her direction. She started towards him, trod on an uneven patch of gravel and sharply turned her ankle. Wincing with pain, she supported herself for a moment by the bonnet, rubbing the foot against the back of her other leg.

'Good Lord!' exclaimed a very familiar deep voice. 'What the devil are you doing here?'

Gina turned surprised eyes to find herself looking into the startled face of Russell Steele. 'Oh!' she breathed, '*You!* I—I've been following your tail-lights . . . but I didn't realise it was you. Think I must be lost. Where are we?'

'You happen to be in my drive,' he retorted distantly. 'This is Hambledon Crescent . . . Highgate. Where did you think you were?'

Why did the wretched man always manage to catch her at a disadvantage? She wouldn't put it past him to imagine that she'd followed him on purpose. 'I—I thought it was Golders Green,' she stammered, mortified. 'C—could you point me in the right direction?'

Trying her injured foot on the ground, she caught her bottom lip between her teeth.

'What's the matter . . . are you in pain?' he demanded.

'Just ricked my ankle . . . it'll go off in a minute.'

'You'd better come inside and let me have a look at it.'

'Honestly, it's nothing,' she protested. 'If you'll . . .'

'Don't argue,' he snapped. 'Can you walk?'

'I—I think so . . .'

He took her elbow and she limped along beside him towards a large pillared portico where he put his key into the heavy front door.

It opened into a brightly lit oak-panelled hall, carpeted in soft green and furnished with a telephone table and a long upholstered settle. Motioning her to sit down Russell dumped his brief-case on the floor and peeled off his driving gloves. Then, kneeling in front of her, he unlaced her flat walking shoe and took her black-stockinged foot in his hands.

His touch sent an animal excitement racing through her veins, despite the discomfort as he twisted her ankle this way and that. Even so she was filled with an odd sense of the ridiculous, gazing at the top of his bent head with the deep dark waves of his hair moist from the fog. She restrained the urge to giggle. It was certainly no laughing matter to have put herself under an obligation to him.

'Well, it doesn't seem too bad to me,' he said,

comparing the foot with her sound one.

'I told you so.'

'It'll probably swell a bit. I could strap it for you.'

'No thanks, I'll . . .' She broke off as she became aware of a stately, silver-haired lady coming down the wide curving stairway which led off the hall.

'Good gracious, Russell,' the woman said with a laugh in her well-bred voice. 'That's something I never thought to see . . . you kneeling at the feet of a pretty girl!'

He stood up and smiled at her. 'Hallo, Mother. This is Gina Brent, one of our nurses. She seems to have lost her way in the fog . . . and she's sprained her ankle.'

'Oh dear, is it bad?'

'No, nothing serious,' Gina hastened to assure her.

'Well, that's a relief. It's a shocking night, isn't it? Have you far to go?'

'It seems I'm way off course,' Gina said, 'but if Dr Steele can put me on the right road . . .'

'You'd probably finish in a pile-up . . . or in someone else's drive,' he cut in satirically. 'I don't think I dare let you loose on an unsuspecting public.'

His mother laughed. 'Really, Russell, you mustn't be so disparaging.' She turned to Gina. 'Take no notice of him, my dear. It only means he's concerned for your safety.'

'Well, thank you . . . but what am I going to do then?' Gina's forehead creased in perplexity. 'The fog might not clear for ages, and I can't impose . . .'

'You'll just have to stay the night,' Russell decided impatiently, 'I don't want a corpse on my
conscience.'

Mrs Steele beamed from one to the other. 'Yes,
I'm sure that's best. I'll go and tell Edna there's
another for dinner.' She disappeared through one
of the doors leading off the hall.

'I'm so sorry to be a nuisance.' Gina stole a timid
glance at the doctor's stern face as she replaced her
shoe and loosely retied the lace. 'And I haven't got
so much as a toothbrush with me,' she added with
an attempt at levity.

He didn't smile. 'Is there anyone you should let
know where you are?'

'No . . . my flatmate went home for the day . . .
she won't be back until tomorrow. Could I get my
handbag from the car?'

'I'll get it. Can't risk you turning your other
ankle. Where is it?'

'It's on the front seat,' she told him in a small
voice.

His mother reappeared. 'That's all right then.
Edna says no problem, the meal will stretch to
three. Shall I take your coat? And there's a cloakroom over there if you'd like to tidy up. Then come
on into the living-room.'

Well, at least she was being gracious about it,
thought Gina, even if her son was acting like a
bad-tempered bear. He returned with her bag and
she went to the cloakroom trying not to hobble too
noticeably.

Looking in the mirror to comb her hair, she felt
very workaday in her striped uniform dress,

although the neat white collar gave her a demure appearance and the silver-buckled navy belt accentuated her trim waist. Her white apron she had discarded when being fitted for the Sister's uniform. With a small sigh of resignation she smoothed her skirt and went out to join the others, pushing open the door to the living-room somewhat hesitantly.

'Come in and make yourself at home,' invited her hostess cheerfully.

'Thank you,' Gina smiled and seated herself in one of the deep-cushioned leather armchairs. The room had a welcoming atmosphere with its warm gold carpet and rich brown velour curtains drawn across large windows. At the far end was a polished oak table set with gleaming cutlery and glass on linen place-mats. But there were no feminine touches, like flowers or ornaments; it was distinctly male and uncluttered, apart from a pile of medical journals on top of the bureau.

Russell had followed her in. He had changed his classic grey suit for leisure cords and a light cashmere sweater which added emphasis to his virile masculinity. Taut buttocks, tight stomach, textbook weight—around one-hundred-and-eighty pounds of predatory power. He crossed to the drinks cabinet and she wondered if he had any idea of his sensual appeal.

'Sherry, Mother?'

'Yes please, darling.'

'And for you?' he enquired, briefly turning his head in Gina's direction.

'The same will be fine for me.'

Pouring the drinks, he brought them over before helping himself to a whisky and sitting at the bureau to sort through some post.

'It *is* nice to have some feminine company,' remarked his mother. She went on to gossip about a number of things which soon had Gina feeling more at ease.

'Oh, I don't live here, dear,' she explained when Gina again apologised for having lumbered them with her company. 'My home is in Cornwall. I just invited myself up for a few days while I do some shopping.'

'Rather fortunate, in the circumstances,' interjected Russell, not looking up from his reading.

'Of course we do have some good stores in the West Country,' Mrs Steele rambled on, 'but one can't beat the London fashions. Where is your home, Gina?'

'I grew up in Hampshire, actually. My sister still lives there, but my parents moved to Kensington when Dad's business brought him to London. He travels a lot. He's in the Far East at the moment.'

'And does your mother go with him?'

Gina didn't feel the necessity to explain about the family rift. 'Not always . . . although she has done. At present she's staying with my sister who's expecting her first baby soon.'

'How lovely,' enthused Mrs Steele. 'I wish we'd had daughters. Two sons was all I could manage and neither of them has married yet, so it'll be some time before I can expect a grandchild. By the way, darling,' she said, turning to Russell, 'Fiona rang earlier. She's cross with you for not showing up at her party last night.'

He gave an eloquent shrug. 'I didn't promise. I was too busy as it happened.'

Gina cast her mind back and remembered that he had spent the evening practising for the carol concert, joining everyone in the pub afterwards. Fiona, whoever she might be, was evidently not his number one priority. But that figured. Whereas the majority of the male staff at the hospital were always ready for a light-hearted exchange with anyone in skirts, Russell Steele seemed to go out of his way to discourage anything on a personal level. In the eyes of some that made him all the more intriguing, but in Gina it only prompted an equally cool attitude.

'Oh, come now, there's life outside of work, isn't there, Gina?' remarked his mother brightly.

'I suppose it depends upon the work. Medicine can take you over, if you let it . . .' she reasoned.

The debate was interrupted as a homely, plumpish girl in a brown-and-white check overall, popped her head around the door. 'Everything's ready, my lady,' she said, 'Shall I bring in the soup?'

My lady! The title brought Gina up with a start. So it wasn't plain *Mrs* Steele. And what did that make Russell? Maybe it did explain his detachment . . . maybe his private world was on a different plane to the rest of them.

'Thank you, Edna.' Lady Steele rose and led the way to the dining-table.

Russell pulled out his mother's chair and then

seated Gina to the other side of him. 'I don't usually dine in such style,' he observed, 'but when my mother's here she insists on maintaining standards.'

'Quite right, too,' said Lady Steele. 'You men would be a bunch of savages without the civilising effect of women, wouldn't they Gina?'

Spreading her napkin across her knees, Gina smiled. 'I'm not qualified to say.' She was privately contrasting her own plain attire with the other woman's elegant appearance. The heather-coloured woollen two-piece obviously came from no multiple store. Rings flashed on her well-kept hands and her hair was beautifully groomed. 'Personally I feel very under-dressed for eating out,' she went on ruefully.

Edna came in and set a soup tureen on the table. Serving Gina, Lady Steele commented: 'Oh, but I think that's a most attractive uniform. I'm glad St Benedict's have kept to their traditional style. So much nicer than the modern uniforms, don't you think so, Russell?'

'It's not a subject I lose much sleep over,' he said, seasoning his soup. 'In any case, she's to be changing that one for dark blue quite soon.'

Gina darted him a straight look, wondering if she had imagined the scepticism in his voice. She didn't see why he should take that tone since he himself had been on the selection panel.

But his mother apparently noticed nothing out of place. 'Does that mean you've got promotion? Splendid! Aren't you rather young for such responsibility?'

'I'm not all that young,' said Gina. 'I'm twenty-four. That's about average I should say.'

The doctor's lips twitched. 'Fortunately uniforms make people look much more mature than they really are.'

Edna cleared their dishes and brought in the main course. 'This looks grand,' Lady Steele congratulated her, cutting into the golden pastry of a steak-and-kidney pie. She passed a portion to Gina. 'Help yourself to vegetables . . . I imagine your parents must be very proud of you.'

'I don't know about that,' said Gina with a modest laugh. It wasn't the career my father wanted for me.'

'What had he in mind for you?' Russell's dark eyes showed a gleam of interest.

She didn't altogether welcome this spotlight on herself but an answer seemed to be called for. 'Music,' she said.

'Oh? In what form?'

'I played the violin. I wasn't bad, but I wasn't that talented either. I preferred to keep it as a hobby and earn my living some other way.'

'And why did you choose nursing?' asked Russell's mother.

'Well, I'd always had the inclination, from the time I joined the junior Red Cross,' she explained. 'No one else in our family has any hospital connections.'

'That's rather like Russell,' Lady Steele reflected, 'he's the only doctor in the family. He'd have gone to Sandhurst like his brother if my husband had had his way.'

To Gina's relief the conversation veered away from herself and onto more general topics. As the meal proceeded even Russell seemed to mellow a little in the cordial atmosphere, but at the conclusion he excused himself.

'Sorry I have to leave you . . . I've some work to catch up on that won't wait. Tell Edna I'll have my coffee in the study.'

The two women sat on talking after he had gone. 'You've been awfully kind,' said Gina presently. 'What about the washing-up . . . could I help?'

'Certainly not,' laughed Lady Steele, 'Edna would be most offended. But it is her day off tomorrow, and I'm a late riser, so you may have to look after yourself in the morning. Russell leaves about eight. What time do you want to be away?'

'I could leave at the same time,' said Gina. 'I'm not on until midday, but I'll need to go back to my flat first.' She smothered a yawn.

'You've had a long day, I expect. I'll show you to your room.' Leading the way upstairs, Lady Steele opened a door on the square landing. 'Here you are . . . I think you'll find everything you need.' She crossed to the window and closed the blue print curtains. 'I have enjoyed meeting you . . . sleep well. I'll get Russell to give you a call in the morning,' she promised.

After repeating her thanks, Gina found herself alone and free to take stock of her surroundings. It was a fair-sized room. The modern single bed had a duvet with a pretty print covering to match the curtains. White fitted cupboards occupied the whole of the facing wall with a recessed dressing-table in the centre. In the en suite bathroom fluffy blue towels hung on a stainless steel bathrail. There was soap, talcum, tissues . . . in fact everything for her convenience except a nightdress.

Having bathed, Gina draped her clothes over a chair and slipped naked into bed. She snuggled under the duvet and lay looking around the room for a while, finding it hard to believe that she was there, actually spending the night in the Senior Medical Registrar's house. It was one of those astonishing happenings that sometimes came out of the blue. Her nightmare car-ride had turned into a not unpleasant adventure—but for the fact that it put her in debt to the doctor, which was something she would have preferred to avoid.

But even if he had not seemed too pleased about it at first, his mother couldn't have been more charming. And as he had said, it was lucky she had been there, otherwise things could have been awkward.

Thinking back over the evening it struck Gina that she had told them quite a lot about herself but had learned very little about them; apart from the fact that someone called Fiona seemed to figure in Russell's world.

With her mind working overtime she could not settle to sleep. There was a glossy magazine on the bedside table. Picking it up, she was flipping idly through it when a full-page portrait of a society beauty caught her attention. Gina had no difficulty in recognising the girl. It was the same one she had

seen in the car with Russell. She was posed in an
elegant evening gown, her long fair hair tumbling
about bare shoulders, a deceptive innocence in her
wide green eyes. The caption beneath the portrait
read—*The Hon. Fiona Heppleton-Mallard—one of
this season's most attractive debutantes.*

So *this* was Fiona. Gina studied the photograph
with a degree of irritation. The girl certainly had
poise and was obviously a member of the privileged
classes. Not that that kind of life would appeal to
me, thought Gina. She could think of nothing more
boring than a constant round of parties with fatuous
young men all concerned with being seen in the
right places with the right people. But what was this
girl to Russell? Had she some kind of claim on him?
She might even have slept in this bed . . . this room
did have a feminine flavour.

Gina closed the magazine and switched off the
light, unable to suppress a rising resentment towards this darling of society. Which was a ridiculous state of affairs since Russell's private life was
not the slightest interest to her.

All the same, despite the vibrations of hostility
that sometimes flared between them, there was
something about the man that was hard to resist, a
kind of formidable integrity that commanded her
respect. But it was more than that; his mere presence was enough to spark off a confused mixture
of emotions inside her.

A heavy sigh escaped her as she settled down to
sleep. For no accountable reason she felt restless
and disconsolate. There was nothing she could put
her finger on apart from a vague feeling that her

working world—the one area of her life that presented some kind of stability—was somehow under threat.

CHAPTER FOUR

EARLY next morning a tap on the bedroom doo
awoke Gina. It took her a few moments to remem
ber where she was. 'Yes?' she called and blinke
sleepily when the door opened to admit Russell.

He was clad in a short towelling bathrobe, bar
feet thrust into soft leather slippers, a sprinkling c
dark hairs visible at his bare throat. 'Good morr
ing!' he said briskly, striding in and setting a glass c
orange juice on the bedside table.

'Good morning,' she returned, catching th
pleasant tang of his morning toilet as he movec
Her eyes followed him when he crossed to th
window, swishing back the curtains to let in mor
light.

'The fog seems to have cleared but it still look
pretty grey out there,' he reported, sizing up th
day. Coming back to her bedside he looked down a
her, hands in pockets, an inscrutable expression i
his dark eyes. His hair curled damply about hi
ears, giving him a boyish charm. She wondered i
he knew the effect he had on women.

'Sleep well?' he asked.

'Yes, thank you.' She smiled uncertainly, unabl
to sit up because of her nakedness and feelin
rather awkward beneath his penetrating gaze.

'How's the foot this morning?'

Under the bedclothes she wriggled it ex

perimentally. 'Seems okay . . . I'd forgotten all about it.'

'Let me see.'

Her colour mounted. 'We—ell, I can't . . . not until I'm dressed.' She tugged the duvet higher about her bare shoulders.

'Oh! Like that, is it?' Dark eyes flickered with amusement. 'It's just gone seven,' he said, consulting his neat gold wristwatch. 'My mother said you wanted to leave when I did. I'll be going at eight . . . I've a clinic this morning. Come down to the kitchen when you're dressed and I'll have toast and coffee ready.'

'The juice will be fine . . . I don't eat breakfast.'

'Everyone should eat breakfast. Don't be too long.' It seemed to imply that she'd eat breakfast whether she wanted to or not!

When he had left her she slid out of bed and tried her foot. Apart from being a little stiff it was not at all bad. Washing and dressing with haste, Gina finally dashed a comb through her burnished hair. Being naturally curly at least that still looked quite decent, even if all she had to wear was yesterday's crumpled uniform.

After carefully straightening the bed, she folded the towels tidily, gathered her things together and found her way down to the kitchen. The room was large and beautifully fitted out with pine cupboards and modern work surfaces. At a round table in the centre Russell sat glancing through his newspaper. He was now immaculately dressed in a dark grey pin-striped suit and crisp pale blue shirt.

Toast popped up from the electric toaster as she

appeared. He motioned her to a seat opposite him and pushed the toast towards her. 'Get on with it,' he prompted, pouring her drink. 'Your waistline won't suffer.'

Obediently she buttered the toast. 'Sorry to have put you to so much trouble,' she said.

He glanced at her from under his straight brows. 'You are, are you? Well, at least my mother seems to have found your company enjoyable.' It inferred that he had not.

'So glad I wasn't a total hang-up,' she murmured with a touch of impudence. What was it about the man that always goaded her to retaliate?

Ignoring her rejoinder he gathered his own breakfast dishes together, putting them in the sink. 'I'll leave you to finish while I collect my things. When you're ready you can follow me in your car until you know where you are.'

She finished her toast, swallowed down the coffee and put her dishes with his in the sink before following him into the hall. Her coat was on the settle where she had left it. He helped her into it, his hands briefly touching the back of her neck, sending a peculiar tingle down her spine.

'Please wish your mother goodbye for me and thank her for being so kind,' Gina said.

He gave a casual nod and they left the house and made for their respective cars.

In the light of day she could clearly see the affluence of the area in which she had passed the night. It was one of the best roads in the vicinity, individually-styled mansions each set in its own landscaped garden.

Russell's house was modern, picturesquely gabled, with a large porticoed entrance. There was a circular drive around a lawned area with a specimen spruce tree in the centre and shrubs of various kinds on either side of the gravelled path. It was a perfect oasis on the outskirts of London.

Her approving eyes taking it all in, Gina could well imagine what a delight it must be to come home to such a place after the busy life of the hospital. Except, of course, that it might be rather lonely when he didn't have guests. Unless he liked to be solitary. On the other hand, he probably didn't lack for company, she decided. Especially feminine company. Maybe Fiona Heppleton-Mallard? Edna, the maid, apparently lived out, so he could do as he pleased without causing any raised eyebrows. Not that he was likely to give a damn about what anyone thought, Gina concluded. She had never known anyone so completely self-assured.

The return journey was much quicker than her hazardous ride of the previous evening. Gina soon began to know where she was. When Russell turned in the direction of the hospital she waved him a cheery goodbye and headed her own car towards the flat.

Mark was about to leave the house when she drove onto the forecourt. 'Hey! What happened to you last night?'

'I stayed with a friend because of the fog,' she explained.

He tutted. 'And there was me getting all worried about you.'

'I don't suppose you even realised I wasn't here,' said Gina with a grin.

'Oh, yes I did. I was all alone. Jason stayed at the hotel and Esther wasn't here either. Anyway, your mum rang . . . I've left a note for you by the box. See you later kid,' and he drove off in his battered red Triumph.

Inside the hall Gina paused by the pay-phone which they all shared and found Mark's note on the message board. She dialled her sister's number and the call was answered by her brother-in-law. 'Hallo, John,' she said, in some surprise. 'What are you doing home at this hour?'

'Parental privilege, Gina. I'm a daddy now, aren't I?'

She squealed with delight. 'Oh! The baby's come?'

'Yes—a seven-pound boy—and he's gorgeous.'

'Oh, that's great! How's Melly? How ~~did~~ she get on?'

'She's fine now, but it had to be a Caesarian, so she'll be in a bit longer than expected. Your mum's here . . . half a mo', I'll pass you over. She'll fill you in on the details.'

Her mother came to the phone and answered all Gina's eager questions. 'I just got home in time, didn't I,' she said.

'You certainly did. But the baby's early . . . I thought Melly had at least a fortnight to go.'

'Oh well, a fortnight one way or the other is neither here nor there.'

'I *must* come down and see you all. It'll only be a flying visit, I'm afraid. I'll check up on my off-duty and see when I can make it.'

'We shall have to let your father know,' her mother went on. 'Have you heard from him lately?'

'Not since the card I had from Bangkok, but he's due home soon, I believe.'

'We'll send a card to the flat.'

'Right . . . and I'll let you know when I'm coming.'

Absolutely thrilled with the family news, Gina's overnight adventure was forgotten for the moment. She hurried along to the general store at the corner of the street to send a greeting to her sister. It was at times like this that she felt out on a limb, not being able to drop everything and dash off to join in the celebrations. Normally her life was so full that she had little time to feel homesick, but not being on the spot to greet the new baby made her feel quite choked.

She shared her excitement with the shop assistant as she chose a suitable card.

'That's nice, dear,' said the woman. 'Nothing like a new baby, is there? Got a nice home to put it in, has she?'

'Oh yes, and a nice husband,' Gina said, addressing the envelope on the counter so that she could post it on the way back.

'She's lucky then. Don't always work out like that, do it?' The woman sounded wistful, as though she might be speaking from bitter experience.

Yes, Melanie was lucky, Gina thought, slipping her card into the letterbox outside. Things didn't always work out. She, too, had known couples who had started off dewy-eyed and ended up going their separate ways before very long. Only recently she'd had news of a schoolmate whose marriage had come adrift. And even her own mother and father, when they should be celebrating their silver wedding, were at crisis-point.

Matrimony could be something of a minefield. Better single blessedness than a doubtful marriage, she mused. She recalled her own heartache at sixteen when her father had forbidden her to get engaged to Chris West, her schooldays' passion. But in hindsight he had been quite right. Chris had gone away to university and their affair had petered out. She had been in and out of love a few times since then, but nothing lasting. At least she had a satisfying career if the right man never came along.

Making herself a snack lunch before going on duty Gina found her thoughts coming back to Russell Steele. That man, he was so maddeningly autocratic she could have yelled at him. And yet she had to admit that in a peculiar sort of way he fascinated her. Purely physical attraction, she decided; that and possibly a bit of pique because of his dismissive manner towards her. And if his kind of girl was the Fiona-type, well, she didn't think much of his judgment. A spoiled social darling would hardly fit in with the busy life of a hospital doctor.

'So if I can have my half-day before my day off,' said Gina that afternoon, discussing the off-duty with Sister Lewis, 'I'll be able to shoot down to see the baby.' They studied the rota together and fixed for Gina to have the coming Wednesday afternoon and Thursday. 'I shall have to miss that week's carol practice, but it can't be helped.'

'You'll be arranging all the off-duty yourself before long, Gina,' Andrea reminded her cheerfully. 'That's one thing I'm not going to miss. It's always a problem, trying to please everyone.'

Professor Phipps had escaped from the care of his sister in Wimbledon and was now back at his London flat. 'Our wedding is going ahead as planned, first week in December,' Andrea confirmed. 'I'll be gone by the end of this month . . . but you know the ward as well as I do; you should have no problems.'

'Hope not,' said Gina, 'although I wish I were having to deal with the Professor and not Russell Steele. I always feel as though I'm skating on thin ice with him.'

Sister Lewis expressed surprise. 'Do you? I think he's terrific.'

'Oh, it's just a gut reaction I suppose. We always seem to be crossing swords. I put my foot in it again last night . . .' Gina went on to tell about her misadventure in the fog. 'He wasn't at all pleased, although his mother couldn't have been nicer.'

'Yes, she's a lovely lady,' Andrea agreed. 'I've met both his parents. Sir Richard was a private patient of Perry's. Pots of money in the family. Banking, I think.'

'Mmm, I rather gathered that. I felt like the country mouse last night with nothing to wear but my uniform.'

The arrival of Paul Waring brought an end to confidences. 'Hi, girls!' the surgical registrar breezed, sauntering into the office and perching on a corner of the desk.

He was a long streak of a man with untidy straight brown hair and a drooping moustache outlining his full lips. None of the nursing staff of St Benedict's took Paul too seriously. There was a persistent gleam of devilment in his small hazel eyes and his jokes could wear thin after a while. But to give him his due, his exuberant manner often had a heartening effect on patients.

'Where's this chappie, then? The thrombosis Steele wants me to take over?'

'Mr Trilby, you mean,' said Andrea. She went to the notes trolley and found his file. 'Here you are. Dr Steele has prepared him for losing the foot, so the sooner you can get on with it, the better.' She consulted her watch. 'I've got an appointment so you'll have to excuse me. Gina will look after you,' and she left them to it.

'Right then, sir,' Paul said confidently to Mr Trilby, having made his examination, 'we'll do that for you . . . have you on your feet again in no time.' Giving the patient a cheerful grin, he left Gina to straighten the bedclothes and draw back the curtains.

'You had him almost looking forward to it,' she said with a whimsical smile when she joined him in the office.

Paul sat at the desk scribbling his notes. 'Ah! Mine was the easy part. Steele had the thankless task of breaking the bad news, I'm glad to say.' He closed the file and looked up at her with mischief in his eyes. 'What! No reaction to the mention of our latest superman?'

'What's the usual reaction?'

Paul got up to leave and placed an arm around her shoulders, feigning despair. 'That guy's practically halved my pitch since he arrived.'

'Oh, it takes more than a few muscles to impress me.'

'Good! You've restored my confidence. Hallo, speak of the devil.'

Gina looked to see Russell Steele approaching, together with Peter Smythe.

'I've seen your man, Russell,' said Paul, his arm still resting along Gina's slim shoulders. 'You can transfer him to Paget as soon as you like. So long, Gina. We'll get together sometime.' He tipped her cap forward over her eyes before going on his way.

With a patient sigh she put it straight again and turned her attention to the other two doctors. 'Can I help you?'

For some reason best known to himself Russell Steele was glowering at her. 'If you can spare the time,' he snapped, 'we'd like to do that pleural aspiration for George Morgan. May I see the X-rays?'

Gina produced the films and the doctors studied them carefully on the ward viewer. Having decided on the correct site for tapping the fluid that had gathered around the patient's affected lung, they proceeded to the bedside.

A trolley with the sterile equipment needed had been prepared in advance and throughout the

rather delicate process Gina supported and reassured the apprehensive patient. It all went off
without a hitch.

'That wasn't too bad, was it Mr Morgan?' Gina
said when she had made him comfortable on his
pillows again.

'No,' he replied with relief in his voice.

'Anticipation's usually the worst . . . and you
should feel better for getting all that off your chest,'
remarked Russell, going off to wash his hands.

Peter labelled specimens of the fluid and took
them off for despatch to the path lab while Gina
cleared away the trolley.

The registrar went on to see others of his
patients. He spent a fair time talking with young
Ben, the sixteen-year-old diabetic. The boy was
having hypos at irregular intervals, despite being
well-controlled most times. He was an intelligent
lad, well able to understand the needs of his diet
and to cope with his insulin injections.

'Your blood sugar seems all right now, son,'
Russell told him. 'I hear you had to miss your "O"
levels again. Pity about that.'

'Yes, wasn't it?' said Ben, remarkably cheerful.

'We'll have to see if we can't keep you in good
shape for the next re-sit.'

Back in the office Russell sat down at the desk
and began to plough back through Ben's thick wad
of case notes. 'There must be some reason why he
constantly gets himself into this mess.' He threw an
enquiring glance at Gina who was replacing files in
the notes trolley. 'Any ideas?'

Ben's reaction to missing his exams had made her

think. 'I wonder if his attacks could be self-induced . . . a way of getting out of his exams?' she ventured.

Russell scratched his cheek thoughtfully, his brows narrowing. 'I wonder? He's quite bright enough to figure out how to upset the balance. Let's check.'

Going through the notes they discovered a repeating pattern, the boy's comas coinciding conveniently with exam times. 'Young rascal!' said the doctor with a wry smile. 'I think we shall have to get him some counselling.' He closed the folder and handed it to her, saying pleasantly: 'That was an inspired guess on your part.'

In view of his earlier curtness she felt quite encouraged by the compliment. But she was unprepared when he paused on the way out and asked her casually: 'Are you free tomorrow evening?'

'Er . . . yes, I am. Why?'

'There's a concert on at the Festival Hall. The soloist is playing the Mendelssohn Violin Concerto. I wondered if you'd care to come along?'

It took her breath away. 'You mean . . . with you?'

'Yes.'

She was momentarily speechless before she heard herself saying: 'Why? Has Fiona let you down?'

His mildly friendly expression froze. 'I just thought it might appeal to you, in the light of our recent conversation. Forget it.'

Nettled, he turned to go, but she called him back, ashamed of her own churlishness. 'Russell, I'm sorry. That was stupid of me. I'd love to come . . . if the offer's still open.'

'It was your interest in music that prompted the invitation, nothing more.' There was still a frost in his voice. 'I don't know what time I shall get away from here, but if you like to meet me there, say by the box-office, about seven-thirty?'

'Thank you. Yes, I'd love to.'

The rest of the day passed in a sort of daze as she thought about the impromptu invitation. Whatever adverse undercurrents ran between them, at least they seemed to have a common ground in music. She could not have chosen a better programme herself than one which included the Mendelssohn Concerto; it had always been her favourite.

Back at the house the following evening she was like an excited schoolgirl getting ready for her date. Esther sat on Gina's bed watching as she flipped through her wardrobe. 'Will this be all right . . . what d'you think?' she asked, holding a soft turquoise angora sweater dress under her chin.

'Fine!' said Esther, 'but if there's nothing personal in this date, why are you so bothered how you look?'

Gina grinned. 'That's what he told me . . . but I can always try and change his mind, can't I?'

She decided to wear the sweater dress, tied an apricot-coloured silk square about her throat and sprayed some perfume on her wrists. 'Now I feel like a *femme fatale*,' she said, 'so watch out, Russell Steele.' With a white wool three-quarter length jacket completing her outfit, she set out for the Underground.

In the spacious plant-festooned foyer of the Festival Hall Gina waited, gazing around her with eager curiosity. Visitors thronged the area, a mixed bag of humanity flowing up and down the broad staircases leading to various levels of the concert hall. Presently she caught sight of Russell approaching her, slipping off his sheepskin jacket on the way. A ripple of admiration ran through her at the sight of him. His broad-shouldered lissom body was enough to turn any girl's head, she thought.

'Hallo!' she said, with a shy smile.

'Sorry if I've kept you waiting. I had difficulty finding a parking spot. We've still time for a drink, though.' Taking her arm, he led her to the bar.

'Are you a regular here?' Gina nibbled the olive from her Martini, eyes bright with anticipation of the treat ahead.

Leaning against the counter, he regarded her with a lazy benevolence. 'I wouldn't say that. Why, are you?'

'No. The last time I was here was for last year's carol concert. Have you taken part in it before?'

He shook his head. 'This year will be a first for me.'

'Oh, you'll enjoy it. There's a great atmosphere.'

'Something like the end-of-term celebrations, I presume?' he said with a condescending smile.

She felt a stab of annoyance at his attitude. It was as though she were a juvenile and he was giving her a night out as a treat. 'There's no need to patronise me,' she retorted.

'Now, now. Don't start getting abrasive again. Let's enjoy the music together, shall we?'

Once more she felt she was being put in her place but she controlled her feelings. 'I'm looking forward to it,' she said levelly.

'That's better.' Taking her empty glass he set it on the counter before guiding her towards the auditorium and their seats.

The concert was a feast of delight for Gina who had all too few opportunities these days for indulging her classical tastes. The violin concerto transported her to a world apart. At the end of the performance she felt heady, refreshed, ready to love everyone.

'That was marvellous. Thank you for asking me, Russell,' she said as he helped her on with her coat.

'My pleasure. I'm glad you enjoyed it.' He suggested a coffee when they had left the concert hall and they paused at one of the refreshment bars. 'So you're not sorry Fiona couldn't make it?' he taunted as they carried their drinks to a nearby table.

It brought her down to earth with a bump. Did he have to spoil things by saying that? She didn't know whether he was teasing or whether she really had been just a stand-in. But she was not going to ruin the evening by rising to the bait. She merely smiled and sipped her coffee.

They were amongst the last of the audience to leave the building. Outside on the forecourt the night air was crisp, the sky black and star-studded. Lights swinging along the embankment glinted on the dark waters of the Thames and the face of Big Ben shone out in the distance. Gina turned up her coat collar and thrust her hands into her pockets.

'It's quite a walk to the car,' he said. 'All the regular parks were full up. The one I'm in is a makeshift affair in a back street.'

'Oh, I don't mind a walk. I love London by night. It's a different place, isn't it?'

Briskly they stepped out together, crossing a deserted walkway and going down into the shadowy streets around Waterloo. Their route took them under a grimy railway viaduct. They were some way in when the quietness of the night was shattered by the squeal of brakes. Gina jumped. The noise was followed by what she first thought was a car backfiring. More sharp reports echoed in rapid succession. They both stopped short. A car raced past at the far end of the tunnel. She stared at Russell. 'Wh—what was all that about?'

'It sounded very much like trouble!' Grabbing her hand, he began to run.

Reaching the end of the tunnel they came into a squalid, dimly lit area. There were drab tenements on one side and crumbling hoardings on the other. The place was deserted . . . except for a dark shape which sprawled in the gutter. As they drew nearer Gina caught her breath. It was the body of a man. He lay in a small pool of blood, his features mutilated by a gunshot wound.

'Oh, my God!' she breathed, her eyes wide with horror. She had seen a few gruesome sights in the course of her work, but only in the disciplined, manageable atmosphere of a hospital. This was different. It was as though they were personally involved.

Russell dropped to his knees, feeling for the victim's pulse, sliding his hand inside the man's windcheater, withdrawing it wet with blood.

Detached and calm he glanced up at Gina. 'I'll do what I can. There's a phone-box along there,' he said, pointing, 'dial 999, will you?'

She fled to do as he asked, finding the box some one-hundred yards distant. Alerting the police and ambulance services, she hurried back.

Russell was now on his feet and wiping his hands with his handkerchief. 'Did you get through?'

She nodded, breathing quickly, her heart pounding. Her eyes went to the still body. 'Is he . . . ?'

'I'm afraid so. He was gone before we got here. Must be half-a-dozen bullets in him . . . one through the heart and one clipped the jugular. Will you let me have your scarf?'

Mutely she untied the silk square from her neck and gave it to him. He laid it over the macabre face. 'We shall have to stay here until the police arrive,' he said.

A lone couple paused on the other side of the street, looking curious. 'Want any help?' called the man.

Russell shook his head. 'There's an ambulance on its way.' The couple passed on.

Gina found she was trembling. She turned away, burying her face in her hands, struggling to pull herself together.

He put a hand on her shoulder. 'Are you all right?'

There was the smell of blood on his hand, even though he had wiped it. A shudder went through her. She caught her quivering bottom lip between her teeth as he turned her round to face him.

'Come on,' he encouraged, putting strong arms about her, 'the fellow probably never knew what hit him . . . it was over before we got here.'

Held close against his broad chest, she broke down and sobbed convulsively. It was a few moments before she could compose herself. 'Better now?' he asked.

She nodded, dashing a hand across her eyes.

Taking her woebegone face between his hands he gently kissed her. 'Be brave a bit longer. We'll soon be on our way.'

Flashing blue lights heralded the arrival of the police and shortly afterwards a wailing siren signalled the approach of the ambulance. Russell made his statement, telling what little he knew of the circumstances and after giving his name and address left the officials to their enquiries. With his arm tightly around Gina, he walked her to the dilapidated site of the car park.

Driving home they were both in sombre mood.

'Only young, wasn't he?' said Gina.

'Yes . . . early twenties I should say.'

She shook her head sadly. 'I wonder what they had against him?'

'Gang warfare . . . protection racket . . . some private vendetta?' He shrugged. 'Who knows? It's a twilight world we don't meet up with too often, thank goodness.'

It was almost one o'clock before he pulled up

outside her flat. Switching off the engine, Russell turned to look at her with a doleful expression. 'Sorry our evening had to end like this.'

Gina managed a wan smile. 'Yes, it was a pity. The first part was lovely though.'

'Well, go to bed and try to put the last part out of your mind, eh? Concentrate on the music instead.' He sounded almost paternal. Leaning across, he pushed open the car door for her. 'Goodnight, Gina.' Staying to see her safely enter the house, he gave a slight wave before driving on.

In the downstairs flat all was quiet, Esther having already gone to bed. Stripping off her clothes Gina went to the bathroom and washed thoroughly, trying to rid herself of the clinging smell of blood, trying to shut out the image of the sleazy scene and the pathetic figure in the gutter.

Once in bed she made a valiant attempt to do as Russell had suggested, trying to concentrate her mind on the first enjoyable part of the evening and not the hideous tail-end. But her thoughts insisted on returning to the tragedy and, with it, the memory of Russell's strong, supporting arms.

He had kissed her; not with passion, but in the manner of someone consoling a distressed child. And she realised then that she was in danger of losing her heart to him. She had wanted him to kiss her as a man kisses a woman he loves. But it was clear that he had meant what he said earlier. He had no leanings in that direction. His invitation had been prompted purely by her interest in music.

Tears came, unbidden, once more to her eyes. She wasn't quite sure why. Her mind was in confusion. It was all mixed up with pity for a young life so uselessly ended and a great deal of self-pity because she, too, had succumbed to the powerful appeal of the man she had determined to resist.

CHAPTER FIVE

With her magazine unopened on her lap, Gina gazed out of the carriage window. She had found herself a window-seat in an empty compartment of the Southampton train, but much as she was looking forward to her flying visit to see the family and the new baby, her thoughts at that moment were on Russell Steele.

They had not met since their night out which had ended so dramatically. She thought he might at least have had the decency to find out how she was after the experience. She supposed he might not even notice her absence from the carol practice that Wednesday evening.

Absently she watched last-minute travellers running for the train. Although hearing her compartment door being slid open she did not bother to see who had entered. The burly, bearded young man heaved his hold-all onto the luggage-rack and sat down opposite her, smoothing back his thick sandy hair and taking a paperback from his pocket.

The train jerked forward. Her magazine slid from her lap to the floor. He bent to pick it up and handed it back to her.

'Thank you,' said Gina. She gave him a second look, conscious of a certain curiosity in his eyes.

'Hallo, Gina!' he said with a grin of recognition.

Her blue eyes widened. That wealth of fair hair

topping his rugged features was as she remembered it, but the beard outlining his chin gave a false maturity to his good looks. His green eyes, heavily fringed with fair lashes, sparkled with good humour. 'Chris!' she exclaimed with a light laugh. 'What are you doing hiding behind a beard?'

The train rattled on as they caught up with the events that had patterned their separate lives since they had drifted apart. By tacit consent neither referred to their schooldays romance. Gina learned that Chris was now a lecturer at London University.

'Married?' she asked.

'No. A couple of near misses. How about you?'

She shook her head. 'Too busy for serious relationships.'

'Don't tell me you're a career woman!'

'Well, why not?'

'It's just that I can't see you—little Gina Brent— as a citadel stormer.'

'Not so much of the "little" if you don't mind,' she said with a modest smile. 'Anyway, there aren't too many citadels to storm in the nursing world. It's still predominantly female, although there are lots more men in the profession now than there used to be.'

He looked at her quizzically, a degree of admiration in his eyes. 'I'm amazed you took to nursing. You used to be squeamish. Remember how you passed out that time I got my eye gashed in a Rugby scrum?'

She laughed softly, her gaze straying to the rem-

nant of the scar which still marked his eyebrow.
'I've toughened up a lot since then.'

'Not too much, I hope. Look, when we're back in
town why don't we get together again?'

Gina hesitated for a moment. It had been
pleasant to renew old acquaintance and to talk over
old times but it struck her that she wasn't really
interested in reviving the past. True, he had
aroused her adolescent emotions and she supposed
she would always have a soft spot for him. First love
was sweet, but she felt no rekindling of the old
passion. It had burnt out.

'Yes, why not?' she agreed lightly, 'but not before Christmas though. I've a load of things on
between now and then.'

'There was a time when you would have dropped
everything for the sheer pleasure of being with me,'
he reminded her with a cheeky grin.

She made a face at him. 'Times change!'

They were nearing the end of the journey now
and they settled for exchanging telephone num-
bers. At the terminus they parted after promising
to keep in touch. He made for the University where
he was speaking at a seminar, while she took the
local train to Lyndhurst to be met by her brother-
in-law.

John was still walking on air at being a father.
'Do you want to go home first?' he asked upon
greeting her affectionately, 'or shall we go straight
to the nursing home? Your mum's there, but
they're not all that strict about visitors.'

It was obvious he couldn't wait to show off his
son and Gina, too, was anxious to make the most of

her visit. 'Oh, let's go there straight away,' she said. 'I'm dying to see the baby.'

'Righto!' He took her case and they made for the car.

'Were you with her when they delivered the baby?' she wanted to know.

'Yes . . . nerve-racking business, isn't it? Would it have to be a Caesarian if we had another, do you think?'

'Not necessarily,' Gina answered. 'It could be completely different next time.'

A short ride brought them to the nursing home and there was soon a joyful family reunion around Melly's bed.

Gina crooned over the new infant tucked up in his crib by his mother's side. 'Oh! You're adorable!' she said.

The baby stirred and mouthed his tiny fist. 'You can pick him up and have a cuddle,' said Melly. 'It's nearly his grub-time anyway.'

Gathering the warm bundle against her shoulder Gina felt her throat grow tight. 'You're so lucky, you two,' she murmured.

'*He* wanted a girl first,' her sister joked.

John grinned, holding his wife's hand. 'I'll settle for what we've got. He'll help to keep you women in order.'

'Chauvinist!' accused Gina.

They fell to discussing family likenesses but couldn't agree as to which side of the family the baby resembled. He was to be called Nicholas— since it was nearly Christmas, and Ian after the girls' father.

Back at the house Gina and her mother exchanged news. Laura Brent had a pile of snaps from
her Australian trip. 'I had a lovely time out there,
but I did miss you all,' she admitted. 'It's such a
long way.'

'Did you hear from Dad?'

'Yes, he wrote me once,' her mother said dis-
missively. 'How's your own love-life?'

'Non-existent at the moment,' said Gina. 'Oh!
Remember Chris West?' She went on to tell her
mother about their meeting on the train. '. . . and
my pulse didn't even get into second gear. Funny,
isn't it? When we split up I thought I should die of a
broken heart.'

'So at least your father was right about that,
then?'

'Mmm . . . and with other couples making a hash
of their lives all around me I'm in no hurry to tie
myself down.'

Laura Brent smiled ruefully. 'You mustn't be
influenced by other people's mistakes. Melly and
John are okay.'

'They're the lucky ones. My flatmate Esther had
a rude awakening recently. This guy she's dating
turns out to be married. But she's one of these girls
who feels lopsided without a man. I'm happy doing
my own thing.'

'Why did you come by train?' her mother wanted
to know. 'Nothing wrong with the car?'

'No . . . it's okay, but the weather forecast
wasn't good and I couldn't afford to be fog-bound
up here.' She gave a graphic account of how she had
come to spend the night at Russell Steele's house.

'Lady Steele?' Laura Brent queried. 'That name rings a bell. Your father and I met a Sir Richard and Lady Steele at that business convention we went to in the States last year. 'Can't be two of them. They were a very distinguished-looking couple. What's the son like?'

'Tall, dark and handsome . . . and knows it,' said Gina wryly. 'Everyone swoons at the sight of him, with the exception of me.'

Her mother smiled. 'And I suppose *you* get the urge to cut him down to size. I know the feeling. That's the way I used to react to your father. Maybe I should have left it at that after all.'

'Oh, don't be ridiculous. I give up on you two,' sighed Gina.

Her visit went all too quickly. The following day she and her mother spent a morning in town shopping. Gina bought a fluffy blue sleeping bag for her new nephew and a bouquet of pink long-stemmed roses for her sister. She also took the opportunity to buy a dress for herself for the nurses' ball.

'Wow!' said John admiringly when she displayed the midnight-blue chiffon gown for his approval. 'You'll be a knockout in that. Got a partner for this gig . . . or would you like me to do the honours?'

'Thanks all the same,' Gina laughed, 'but *your* place is pacing the midnight floor with junior from now on. Actually I'm taking Mark . . . he's the dental student in the flat upstairs . . . and, no, we haven't got anything going.'

There was just time for a final visit to the nursing home that afternoon before her mother drove her back to Southampton to catch the London train.

'I'll be sending your ticket for the carol concert,' Gina promised as they said goodbye. 'You can stay overnight at our place . . . or will you go back to Kensington?'

'I'll stay with you, love, if that's convenient.'

'Yes, of course it is. Jason's gone to Paris . . . he won't mind you borrowing his bed.'

Arriving back in London to a damp and murky night, Gina reached the flat at around ten-thirty.

Esther was in the kitchen making herself a night-cap. 'Well, how were they all?' she wanted to know.

'Great!' Gina launched into a glowing account of her sister and the baby. 'How did the carol practice go yesterday?' she enquired presently.

'Fine! We had our usual binge at the pub afterwards. He wanted to know where you were,' Esther added.

'But I told Peter why I wouldn't be there . . .'

'Not *Peter*. Russell asked me.'

'Did he?' Gina's pulse quickened. 'Oh, he probably thought I wasn't pulling my weight, I suppose.'

'No, I told him where you'd gone. He seemed interested. He said you'd mentioned that your sister was about to produce.'

Gina opened up her case and took out her new dress. 'I got this for the ball while I was there. Like it?'

With a show of enthusiasm Esther fingered the rich, silky chiffon, but Gina thought her friend seemed rather despondent. 'Is everything all right with you?' she queried.

'Oh, it's just that I'm through with Graham,

that's all. I woke up to the fact that it's a mug's game, being the other woman.'

'You're right there.' Gina sighed sympathetically as Esther chewed her lip. 'Sorry, but it was best to make the break before you got too involved. He wanted the best of both worlds . . . slippers by the fire and nights on the tiles as well. Anyway, he wasn't nearly good enough for you.'

'Which leaves me without a partner for the ball on Saturday. And no Jason to fall back on either,' Esther said mournfully.

'Never mind. You can share Mark with me. Or, wait a minute, I've got a better idea. I met an old mate of mine on the train going down. His name's Chris West. I'm sure you'd like him. He gave me his phone number . . .' She searched in her diary. 'I'll see if he's free.' But there was no reply when Gina rang. 'I'll get on to him first thing in the morning,' she promised.

Although she was not on duty until midday she set her alarm for eight-thirty to be sure of catching Chris before he went in to college.

'That was quick,' he cracked. 'I thought I'd be hearing from you sooner or later, but this is rather sooner than even I expected.'

'Well, don't let it go to your head,' she returned. 'The thing is, my flatmate's partner has had to opt out for our annual ball on Saturday, so there's a ticket going spare if you'd like to come. How about it?'

'Oh, I see. I'm not awfully keen on blind dates.'

'Listen,' Gina cut in, 'this'll be the best blind date you ever had. Esther's great.'

'Okay. I'll do it just for you.'

'Thanks, Chris. It's at The Grosvenor. We'll meet you in the foyer there, six-thirty for seven. 'Bye.'

Esther had already gone in to work and with a feeling of satisfaction at having been able to fix her up with a partner Gina went back to bed for a couple of hours. She lay in a state of blissful idleness, musing on the events of the past two days and rather pleased to think that Russell had noticed her absence. So at least she must have made some kind of impression on him, no matter how indifferent he might appear.

At one o'clock Gina was back at the hospital and taking over from Sister Lewis. It was Andrea's last weekend. She gave a comprehensive report and some good advice to help Gina in her role as sister.

There had been a couple of admissions in her absence. A Mr Chesham, transferred from ITU was recovering from a cardiac arrest, and there was also an attractive youngish man with a slipped disc. 'The orthopaedic wards were full up,' Andrea explained, 'so we've got him for the time being. He's on traction and having i.v. Valium for the pain. By the way, I should keep your eye on young Sharon Evans. She's a bit of a shirker. I heard her moaning about having to do all the donkey work. I had to remind her that we've all done our share of that.'

'Too true!' Gina smiled reflectively. She hadn't forgotten what it was like to be a first-year student. Her gaze went through the office window to where Sharon was collecting urinals in a lackadaisical fashion, her lank fair hair flopping untidily about her face. She made a mental note to try to encourage the girl.

Andrea rolled down her sleeves and prepared to go off-duty. 'You'll look in at the Dean's farewell party for Perry and me tonight, won't you? It's in the Residents' Dining Room.'

Gina promised that she would. 'It's going to be quite a weekend, what with that and the ball tomorrow. Will you be there?'

'No, we're having to give the ball a miss. Perry mustn't overdo it.' Taking her bag from the staff cupboard, Andrea paused to pick up a bulky manilla envelope. 'This came for you,' she said, passing it over. 'I'll be off then. See you later.'

Glancing briefly at the package, Gina thought at first it was from Admin, dealing with her new contract of employment. She was about to put it aside to study later when a certain softness about the contents struck her as unusual. Curiosity getting the better of her, she opened the envelope straight away. Inside it was a Harrod's bag, and inside that was an exquisite pure silk square. It was soft apricot in colour, similar to the one she had parted with to cover the murdered man's face. Enclosed with it was a visiting card on which Russell Steele had scrawled: 'With my compliments.'

Shaking out the scarf with a smile of surprise, she glanced up to find the donor about to enter the office. 'Hallo!' she said, 'Thank you for this. It's lovely. But you really shouldn't have bothered. Mine was only a cheap polyester job.'

He accepted her thanks with a careless shrug.

'Well, I don't know much about these things. Fiona did the shopping for me. Is the colour right?'

'Yes, perfect,' she said, but the mention of Fiona somehow spoiled her pleasure.

'I want to take a look at your new cardiac patient,' he went on without wasting time.

'Mr Chesham. Yes, his notes are here.' She handed him the folder from the desk. 'Sister Lewis says he seems to be stable. He sat out of bed this morning to have it made. I haven't talked to him yet myself.' (Why did he always manage to jump in on her before she'd had a chance to catch up on ward affairs?)

The patient in question was in a bed near the office so that he could be kept under observation in case of any sudden change. Now Gina accompanied the doctor to see him, drawing the curtains around his bed and giving him a warm smile.

'Hallo, Mr Chesham. Any problems?' asked Russell, his fingers closing over the radial pulse, his perceptive eyes making careful observation of the patient's demeanour.

'Just a bit breathless, Doctor.' Mr Chesham was an average-sized man in his fifties with thinning brown hair. At first sight he looked fairly healthy but he had a history of rheumatic fever and he had been a life-long smoker. 'What wouldn't I give for a ciggy,' he sighed. 'I suppose that's out of the question now?'

'Well, it would certainly be advisable to cut it out if you can.' Russell applied his stethoscope to listen to the heart sounds. 'That seems fairly satisfactory,' he said reassuringly. 'We'll get another ECG done to monitor how things are going. All being well we shan't need to keep you in much longer, providing you're sensible when you go home. Not too much riotous living over Christmas.'

Gina stayed to tidy the bedclothes and exchange a friendly word with the patient while Russell returned to the office to write up his observations and instructions for tests.

'He seems rather anxious,' he remarked when she rejoined him. 'I've written him up for Diazepam as necessary. Keep the fluid chart going . . . how was your sister?' he asked, suddenly looking up from his writing.

'Oh, fine, thank you.'

'What did she have?'

'A boy. 7-lbs. He's gorgeous.'

There was a dreamy note in her voice and Russell eyed her with amusement. 'Why does a new infant make all other women feel broody?'

'Who's feeling broody?' Gina returned sharply. 'I can enthuse over a baby without necessarily wanting one.'

'Yes, if you say so,' he conceded with an irritating smirk, 'but I should have thought you were just as prone to the biological urge as any female.' He closed the folder, handed it to her and left, suppressing a grin.

Gina clutched the notes fiercely, watching him go. She felt like throwing them after him. '*Condescending clown*' she muttered beneath her breath. She didn't know how she could have imagined she might be falling for him. He was impossible. But there was no time to waste brooding over such trifles. Nurse Wynford was not yet back from lunch and there was the drugs round still to be done.

In the sluice Sharon was sterilising a bedpan as Gina passed to unlock the drugs trolley from its station behind the equipment room. She remembered her resolve to try and encourage the student. 'Would you like to do the drugs with me when you've finished there?' she called in a friendly manner.

'All right,' returned the girl with scant enthusiasm. She washed her hands in a dilatory fashion before joining Gina at the trolley.

They worked their way around the ward, taking each patient's treatment sheet in turn and looking up the prescribed medication. Gina explained the purpose of the various treatments which had been ordered and checked dosages of the drugs before they were given. Halfway through the round she was called to the telephone. When she returned she found the trolley unattended and Sharon some way off flirting with the patient with a slipped disc.

Calling her back, Gina murmured in mild reproof: 'Sharon, surely you know that the drugs trolley must *never* be left unattended?'

'Of course,' said the girl carelessly. 'I was keeping my eye on it.'

'You could hardly do that with your back to it. You should have locked it if you were going to leave it. Watch it in future. We should all have been for it if something had gone missing.'

Sharon adopted an air of injured innocence. The

round was finished without further incident and the trolley safely restored to its place.

'Okay, wash up the medicine glasses and then you can take your break,' said Gina ignoring the girl's hostile attitude. But watching her dawdle off in the direction of the sink, Gina sighed. With the best will in the world Sharon Evans was a difficult girl to help. She didn't take kindly to advice or instruction and her know-all attitude certainly didn't go down well with the rest of the staff. Fortunately she would be moving to another ward before long, but Gina had her doubts as to whether she would stay the course.

Visiting time came and went. Suppers were served, patients confined to bed were washed and their pressure areas treated before the night staff came on.

It was after nine before Gina was free to join the Dean's farewell party for Sister Lewis and Professor Phipps. In the staff room she discarded her uniform for jeans and a sweater and freshened up with a quick wash before making her way down to the Residents' Dining Room. It was crowded with medical and senior nursing staff and a buzz of chatter and laughter greeted her ears.

In pride of place on a centre table stood the presentation silver salver complete with crystal champagne glasses.

Depositing her bag and coat on a chair near the door, Gina went over to offer her good wishes to Andrea and the Professor. 'St Benny's won't be the same without you,' she said.

The Professor's keen eyes twinkled. 'At least

we're leaving Harvey Ward in good hands, as I can vouch from personal experience.' He beckoned to Russell, standing nearby. 'There you are, m'dear fellow. The old firm and the new, eh? I was just saying what a splendid ally you'll have in this young lady.'

'I think we shall rub along,' conceded Russell with a one-sided smile.

'Good! You take her away now and find her a drink.'

Shepherding Gina towards the bar, Russell seemed to be in a sociable mood. She asked for a lager and helped herself to some crisps while he poured it. Others milled around them and there was a lively exchange of banter.

Paul Waring bounced over, greeting Gina with a kiss. He seemed even more fulsome than usual and she suspected he had been imbibing quite freely.

'Have you been knocking it back?' she said, laughing.

'Me, dear heart? What a suggestion! I'm no-where near my capacity. Come on, drink up. Have a vodka?'

'No thanks. I'll stick to lager.'

He ruffled her red-gold curls. 'Why don't you let that beautiful hair down? I've been waiting for a chance to get to know you when you're uninhibited.'

The Dean called for their attention while he delivered a wordy tribute to the Professor and his bride-to-be. Gina rested her glass on the bar to join in the general applause.

Furtively tipping his glass of vodka into her lager,

Paul winked slyly at Russell, but the senior medical registrar was unamused. 'I don't think that was very clever, old chap,' he said.

'Sshh!' murmured Paul, laying a finger against the side of his nose. 'It wasn't much anyway.'

'No?' Russell looked disapproving and wandered off to join another group.

'What was all that about?' said Gina, looking after him.

'Couldn't say,' replied Paul, all innocence. 'Have some peanuts?'

She took a handful from the dish he offered and afterwards drained her glass.

'It'd be a miracle if *he* ever let *his* hair down,' she muttered, gazing at Russell's broad shoulders across the room. And the thought of Russell with long hair made her rather giggly.

Paul's eyes gleamed. 'Feeling happy?'

'Mmm!' she said. 'There's something about weddings that gets me here.' She laid a hand on her chest and looked at him with large, solemn eyes.

'Gets you there?' he repeated, laying his own hand over hers.

She pushed it away. 'Paul . . . don't do that . . . not in front of everyone.'

'All right, let's go outside then,' he whispered with his arm around her.

Gina shook her head in mock despair. 'Don't you ever give up? Still, I suppose every hospital has one.'

'Has one what?'

'A guy who thinks he's irresistible to all women.' She grinned at him, feeling delightfully carefree for some reason, her end-of-day tiredness gone.

All was free-and-easy in the off-duty atmosphere. Portraits of past surgeons and physicians gazed down with solemn faces on the cordial assembly.

Gina's conversation sparkled. Paul plied her with another lager which he had surreptitiously treated as before. 'This must be my last,' she said, 'I've got to drive home.'

He looked a little startled. 'You're driving? Come back to my room for a black coffee first.'

She laughed. 'You must be joking. Go and find some little first-year to seduce. I'll have to be leaving though, I'm on an early tomorrow.'

'You sure you're all right to drive?' he asked anxiously.

'A darned sight safer than I would be drinking coffee with you.'

He followed after her as she went to pick up her coat and bag. 'Look Gina, hang about. I—I . . .'

'Go away!' she told him firmly.

'You heard what the lady said,' Russell interrupted.

She seized the opportunity to slip away, leaving the two men talking and Paul looking decidedly worried.

Her legs began to feel oddly feeble as she went in search of her car. And all I had was a couple of lagers, she thought, muddle-headed as she felt in her pocket for her keys. Perhaps it was because she hadn't eaten much. Finding the keys she searched for the right one and attempted to fit it into the lock, dropping the bunch in the process.

'Damn!' she murmured, groping for them among the damp leaves that had collected by the kerb.

Running footsteps caught up with her. 'What have you lost?' said a deep voice.

'My keys. Oh, here they are.' Triumphantly she pounced upon them and stood up to find Russell towering above her. 'Hallo! You again?' She beamed at him before trying once more to select the right key while he stood watching with narrowed eyes. 'Oh dear! I'm all fingers and thumbs tonight.' Giving him a sweet smile, she handed the keys to him. 'You do it for me.'

He dropped them back into her coat pocket. 'That's not all you are,' he retorted bleakly. 'You're certainly not fit to drive. Come on, I'll take you in my car.' Slipping an arm through hers, he guided her in the direction of his Jaguar.

For a change she did not feel in the least put out by his peremptory manner. In fact she felt quite flattered. It was probably just his way of saying that he wanted to take her home, she concluded. So perhaps he did fancy her after all. And he certainly was rather gorgeous.

Sitting in the car beside him, stealing glances at his stern profile, she had an overwhelming urge to penetrate that controlled detachment. There was something about his purposeful self-restraint that tantalised her.

'Don't look so grim, Russell,' she said in a soft persuasive voice, 'anyone would think you had a time-bomb on the seat beside you instead of just me.'

He concentrated on the road. 'I couldn't think of a more apt description,' he retorted.

'Are you flirting with me?' she suggested hopefully.

'I rather think the boot's on the other foot.'

'Well, you would say that, wouldn't you? Because you're used to having women fall over you.'

'But not you, as a rule,' he returned with a ghost of a smile, bringing the car to a halt outside her flat. 'Will you be all right now?'

She looked up into his frowning face with a winsome smile, feeling absurdly reckless. 'You can kiss me if you like. I don't mind.'

He leaned back in his seat, his dark eyes studying her closely in the light of the street lamp, but he made no move towards her.

'All right, don't then. As if I care!' She knew the thing to do was to storm out of the car, but she sat there biting her thumbnail, chastened at his rejection.

Russell curbed a grin. He drew her lazily towards him. 'I warn you, you're going to regret this in the morning,' he said.

Her lips parted as he bent to kiss her. Her body moulded to his, warm and submissive. She had an intense longing to give herself completely, to sweep away the conventions of her moral upbringing. His mouth became more demanding, his embrace more passionate. Her desire amounted to uncontrollable proportions as she was drawn even closer to him. Then, unexpectedly, he thrust her sharply away.

'Time you were in bed,' he barked. 'I'll see you in.'

Tears pricked her eyes. 'I—I thought you wanted me . . .' she said, bewildered. Her head was reeling. She couldn't make sense of anything. Somehow she appeared to have made a dreadful mistake. Oh, how utterly humiliating!

He got out of the car and came round to open her door as she fumbled with the lock.

'I can m—manage,' she mumbled, pushing aside his helping hand with an attempt at dignity.

She stood up, but her legs threatened to telescope. He put a supporting arm around her waist and she made it as far as the front door before she crumpled altogether, laying against him like a rag doll.

'Where's your door key?' he demanded, but she closed her eyes, past caring.

With a sigh he searched in her pocket, found the key on her bunch and opened the door. Scooping her up in his arms, he carried her inside.

Esther appeared in the doorway of her room, clad in her dressing-gown and holding a mug of coffee. Her eyes popped. 'What the . . . ?'

'Sorry to barge in like this, but your friend is plastered,' Russell explained. 'Where do you want her?'

'In here.' Hastily Esther showed him to Gina's bedroom where he deposited her on the bed.

'Probably best just to let her sleep it off.'

'Gina sloshed?' Esther gazed at him in amazement. 'But she hardly drinks at all!'

He gave a short brittle laugh. 'I can well believe you. Some joker laced her drink with vodka while her back was turned.'

'Couldn't you have warned her if you saw what was going on?' flared Esther.

Russell shrugged. 'Maybe I should have, but I wasn't to know she couldn't take it. In any case I didn't realise how much she'd had until it was too late.'

'Well, thanks for bringing her home, anyway.'

'It was the least I could do.' He scratched his cheek as he studied the slight figure flaked out on the bed. 'She's going to have a thick head in the morning. If she wants to know where her car is, it's still at the hospital. I'll leave you to look after her, then. Goodnight.'

'Goodnight,' said Esther. 'Thanks again.'

She left him to see himself out while she loosened Gina's clothes and took off her shoes. 'Gina!' she called, giving her friend a little shake, 'come on, let's get your things off.' But Gina simply grunted and curled herself up, leaving Esther no alternative than to cover her with the quilt and let her sleep it off as Russell had advised.

Four specially selected
Doctor Nurse Romances – FREE

In the high-pressure life of a busy hospital, people find themselves unexpectedly drawn together. Perhaps it's the daily tragedies and ordeals of working with the weak and helpless, perhaps it's the shared satisfaction of a difficult job well done — whatever the causes, people find themselves involved not only with their work... but with each other.

Send today for your Four Free Books, and reserve a Reader Service Subscription for eight brand new Doctor Nurse Romances every two months, delivered to your door postage and packing free. And you can enjoy many other advantages:

 No commitment — you receive books for only as long as you want.

 Free newsletter — keeps you up-to-date with new books and book bargains.

 Helpful friendly service from the girls at Mills & Boon. You can ring us anytime on 01-684 2141.

A subscription to Doctor Nurse Romances costs just £8.00 every two months, but send no money now — these four books are yours to keep — **FREE.**

You have nothing to lose — fill in the coupon today.

CHAPTER SIX

'TIME to get up, Gina!' Esther planted a mug of coffee on her friend's bedside cabinet and sat down on the bed, waiting patiently.

Gina stirred, muttered, and turned over.

'Come on, it's gone six,' Esther said firmly, 'Time to be moving.'

With a weary yawn Gina stretched, opened her eyes, then shut them tightly again, clutching at her temples. 'Ooh! I've got a splitting head,' she groaned.

'I'm not surprised, the state you were in last night.'

'What d'you mean . . . the state I was in?' Gina frowned, casting her mind back to the previous evening. 'I had a couple of lagers, that's all.'

'That's what *you* thought. A little bird told me someone filled you up with vodka.'

'*What?*' Gina propped herself up on her elbows and stared at her flatmate in dismay, trying to remember what had happened at the party. She had only hazy recollections. Paul Waring had been there, his usual reprobate self, inviting her to his flat with that suggestive gleam in his eyes. But surely he wouldn't . . . would he? Yes, he would. '*Paul Waring!* Wait till I see that louse,' she muttered, striving to piece together the course of events.

'That figures,' said Esther with a disparaging laugh, 'Were you with him?'

'Yes, but . . .' She knew she hadn't gone back with him to his flat, because she could remember dropping her keys in the car park. And Russell had been there. After that things were obscure, except for the wild dreams that had haunted her sleep. Unless . . . 'Esther, how did I get home?' she queried anxiously.

'Russell brought you. Carried you in bodily, as a matter of fact. Your car's still at the hospital, so you'll have to come in on the bus with me this morning.'

There was mounting horror on Gina's face. She ran a hand through her dishevelled curls, noting for the first time that she was still partially dressed. 'Oh help!' she groaned, 'I thought I'd been having a nightmare. I was in this car making love to him. It couldn't have been for real, could it?'

Esther shrugged and laughed. 'If it had been Paul who brought you home, yes. But anything's possible. You'll have to ask him. All I know is that I hardly slept a wink. I kept coming to have a look at you, just in case you were sick or something.'

'Oh God! I'm sorry. How awful.' Gina was devastated. 'I could kill that rat Waring. Oh! My head.'

'Drink your coffee and take a couple of Panadol. You'll feel better once you get moving.' Esther giggled. 'I wonder what you really got up to last night?'

She departed to get herself ready for work, leaving Gina to agonise over the unknown. So Russell had brought her home. She had been in a car with him; that part wasn't a dream. But had she actually made love to him, or had that been just a figment of her imaginings? She really must have been past it if he'd had to carry her in! How was she ever going to be able to face the man again?

Searching in her drawer for a couple of pills she swallowed them down with her drink before going to the bathroom. A shower did help to revive her physically but did nothing to ease her distress at having to be brought home incapable; and by Russell Steele of all people.

The air was crisp and fresh as the two girls stepped out towards the bus-stop. It helped to clear Gina's head. 'Thank goodness I'm on a half-day,' she said, 'I shall have a sleep this afternoon or I won't be much of an asset at the ball tonight. Wait till I catch up with that idiot Paul!'

But Paul was not in evidence that morning and, much to Gina's relief, there was no sign of Russell on her ward either. Her period of duty passed uneventfully with the routine of the ward proceeding smoothly. She did wonder if her lapse would have circulated on the grapevine, but no-one made any comment. Before going off-duty she lunched with Esther and Zoe Wynford in the canteen.

'So it'll be the sisters' dining-room for you after today,' Zoe reminded her. 'Look your last on the lower-deck.'

'Yes, you're right.' Gina felt a twinge of regret at the prospect of moving on from the familiar surroundings where she had shared meals and ex-

changed gossip with the friends she had ma
during her training.

Tomorrow would be her first official day as sist
of Harvey Ward. She was going to miss t
matiness of the students. Looking around thoug
fresh faces were appearing all the time. And a st
up the ladder meant that you were not expected
mix quite so freely with all and sundry. She was w
aware that the efficient running of a ward stemm
from the top and you could hardly fraternise o
moment and give orders the next. Andrea Lev
had been a good example. Friendly and approac
able, yet demanding a high standard of care fro
her staff.

'Oh well,' Gina went on more brightly, 'You
both be joining me there before too long, I expec'

Back at the house she went to bed and tried
sleep but she was still plagued by thoughts of t
previous evening. The whole affair was so degra
ing. True, she had been the innocent victim of
practical joke; Russell could hardly blame her f
that. The trouble was people did all kinds of m;
things when they were tight. She hoped she had
made a fool of herself.

By the time Esther arrived home Gina h;
washed her hair and bathed and had recover
from her morning hangover. They were havi
coffee together when Mark came in from a sho
ping expedition.

'Hi, girls!' He dumped his packages on the floc
straddled a kitchen chair and leaned his arms on t
back. 'Just what the doctor ordered, a nice cupp
I've been trailing around buying me a velvet bow t

for tonight, and a new shirt. Decided I'd better be a credit to you.'

'That'll be the day!' said Gina. Taking another mug from the dresser, she made him coffee. 'How shall we go tonight . . . your car or mine? My friend Chris is meeting us there.'

'Oh, let's take a taxi . . . do things in style,' Mark decided. 'I'll pay.'

Esther's eyes widened in mock surprise. 'The moths in your pocket will die of shock.'

'We'll let that pass,' he said magnanimously. 'All I've got in my pocket are holes. Actually I had a nice cheque from my doting grandfather this morning so I'm feeling flush. And if we're not driving no need for any of us to stay on the wagon.'

'*I* shall probably stay on the wagon anyway,' said Gina.

'You touched a nerve there. She got taken for a ride last night,' Esther told him, explaining.

Mark hooted with laughter. 'This guy who brought you home was onto a good thing, wasn't he? A defenceless bird at his mercy?'

Gina aimed a lump of sugar at him. 'I wasn't *that* defenceless. And he's a man of principle, I hope,' she added as Mark hooted with laughter again. 'Oh, push off and get ready. Time's getting on and I told Chris we'd meet him at six-thirty.'

The mini-cab they ordered duly collected them and dropped them at The Grosvenor. Chris was there in the foyer waiting. He looked extremely stylish in his dinner-jacket, his thick fair hair gleaming gold in the subdued lighting, his beard emphasising his determined chin.

Gina made the introductions and after a few moments of light exchanges the girls went to the cloakroom.

'First impressions favourable, Esther?' said Gina as they waited to hand in their coats.

'Mmm . . . quite tasty. I'm surprised you don't want to keep him for yourself.'

'No, ours was only a schooldays' thing. I don't believe in resurrecting ghosts.'

Amid the hum of gossip and the mingled perfumes in the luxurious powder room the girls added last minute touches to their appearance. Gina adjusted the deep-frilled neckline of her dark blue chiffon gown. She was pleased with her choice. The full skirt draped becomingly over her slim hips and the single row of pearls at her throat was the perfect complement.

Esther's dress was ruby-red and figure-hugging, showing her trim figure off to advantage. Her dark brown hair had a rich sheen and her green eyes held a sparkle that had been sadly missing of late.

They joined their escorts and after pre-dinner cocktails followed the throng of people descending the broad, sweeping staircase to the ballroom, brilliantly lit with its crystal chandeliers. Round tables, each seating ten, were arranged around the perimeter of the dance floor. Each was set with a snowy cloth and gleaming cutlery and graced with an artistic centre-piece of flowers.

The table plan was displayed on a stand at the bottom of the stairs. On these occasions it was a hospital custom to mix people up, in order to make for greater sociability. The four of them consulted the plan.

'Here we are. Oh, good, we're with Peter Smythe and his wife,' said Gina with a feeling of relief. She had been half afraid of finding herself at the same table as Russell, or even Paul. She knew that Russell was there because she had spotted his handsome dark head in the distance, but fortunately Paul did not seem to be present.

The four other people on their table were a bio-chemist and his partner and a couple from X-ray. They were not well-known to the girls but they proved to be good mixers and talk flowed easily amongst them all.

At the conclusion of the meal there were the inevitable speeches and toasts to hospital dignitaries before tables were cleared and rearranged to make more space for dancing.

Mark started the evening with Gina and then Chris took her onto the floor for a jiving session.

'Glad you came?' she asked him.

'Yes, agreeably surprised.'

'Do you mean about Esther?'

He gave a guarded smile as he moved his agile body. 'That's a leading question. I meant the atmosphere . . . these official occasions can be horribly stuffy. Your friend is easy on the eye though, I must admit. And what about you, are you still as innocent as you look?' he challenged, his eyes impudently assessing her.

'I didn't exactly go into a nunnery when we lost touch.'

He laughed. 'Maybe I should have hung in there.

One of my youthful errors of judgment. What about Mark . . . is he your steady?'

'No, we just live together.' She laughed as his eyebrows shot up. 'He and his mate have the flat upstairs. Esther and I live on the ground floor.'

'That sounds cosy.'

They fell to talking of old times and mutual friends and were happily at ease with each other before returning to their table at the end of the session.

The band leader was determined to get the company swinging. With a roll on the drums he announced a novelty dance, couples to change partners with the pair nearest to them when the music stopped.

'Come on, Gina, you might meet the man of your dreams. You never know your luck,' said Mark, steering her onto the floor.

'I don't think the man of my dreams exists. And this is a quickstep, not an all-in wrestling match,' she laughed as they careered past other dancers.

The music halted. 'All change!' sang out the compère.

Turning to the couple nearest to them, Gina's heart flipped as they found themselves facing Russell Steele and his partner.

In faultless evening dress Russell looked more striking than ever, with his thick dark hair moulding pleasingly about his ears. And the slim blonde by his side, wearing a model sea-green taffeta gown, was the girl whose picture she had seen in the magazine—Fiona Heppleton-Mallard.

Mark was stabbing his forefinger at Russell's broad chest. 'Hey! Don't I know you? Impacted wisdom tooth, lower jaw. August, wasn't it?'

'Yes, that's right.' Russell smiled in surprise. 'You've got a good memory.'

The music had restarted but their conversation went on. 'Never forget a molar!' Mark breezed. 'How are you?'

'Fine. No trouble at all afterwards.'

Fiona patted a delicate yawn and exchanged a bored glance with Gina. 'Shall we talk amongst ourselves while they do a post mortem on his gnashers?' she murmured.

Mark grinned. 'Sorry, girls. We'll continue this later.' Taking possession of Fiona, he whirled her on, chatting in his ebullient fashion.

Left with Russell, Gina's pulse raced as he looked down at her with some amusement. 'Quite a character, your partner.'

'Yes,' she agreed, focussing her eyes on his snowy shirt-front as he took her into his arms. She was not surprised to find him a good dancer, unlike Mark, whose performance resembled a force-nine gale whatever tune he was dancing to.

'And how are you this evening?' he asked. 'Have you recovered?' The deeply resonant voice sent shivers down her spine.

'Yes, I'm fine.' Forcing herself to meet his steady gaze, she was annoyed to find herself blushing. 'I—I believe I have you to thank for getting me safely home last night.'

His dark eyes gleamed impishly. 'Glad to be of help.'

'I'm afraid I can't remember too much about what happened.'

'Then perhaps we should draw a veil over the proceedings and leave it at that.'

The implication in his tone of voice was not reassuring and she felt she had to know what, if anything, had gone on between them. 'I hope I didn't . . . er . . . embarrass you. I mean, did I say . . . or do . . . anything out of place?'

A muscle worked in his lean cheek. 'Nothing too terrible. Unless inviting me to kiss you was out of place, as you put it?'

So she hadn't dreamt it. It had actually happened. 'Oh dear!' she murmured, 'Sorry about that.'

'No need to apologise. It was quite an enjoyable experience as a matter of fact,' he observed, steering her expertly around a pile-up of couples.

She stiffened and pulled away to look at him. 'You mean . . . you did?'

'How could I refuse such an invitation?'

'Well!' she flashed back, 'Knowing I wasn't in control, *and* through no fault of my own, I think that was pretty contemptible of you.'

He laughed. 'Oh, come on. All right, so I couldn't resist kissing a normally stand-offish young woman. I'm human, aren't I? And I can promise you, your virginity's still intact as far as I'm concerned.'

She flung him a withering glance which made him laugh again and pull her closer. It was a mind-blowing experience, being pressed against his hard, virile body. Unbidden urges raced through her

veins but she fought to suppress them. No doubt he
thought she was fair game now, Gina told herself
darkly. Well, he'd picked the wrong one this time!
He might have the majority of the female staff at St
Benedict's falling over him, but that was not going
to include *her*.

The music stopped on several occasions to allow
people to change partners, but Russell did not play
fair. He carried on dancing with her, enjoying her
discomfiture, so she presumed, the odious wretch.
When he took her back to her table at the end of the
session, they found Fiona sitting there chatting
vivaciously with Mark.

She stopped in mid-sentence and looked up at
Russell as he pulled out a chair for Gina. 'Oh!
You're not going to drag me away, are you dar-
ling?' she said pertly, 'I'm enjoying myself.'

Mark dragged his adoring eyes from Fiona's face
and indicated an empty chair next to Gina. 'Take a
pew for a minute, Russell old man.' Russell seated
himself and leaned back with an air of indulgence
while Mark went on: 'Fiona's been telling me all
about the characters she meets in this Bond Street
gallery where she works. Art, antiques and all that
stuff. I tell you, folks, we're in the wrong racket.
Still, some of us have to serve suffering humanity.'

Chris and Esther came back to the table and
joined in the general debate. Fiona was the centre
of attention, her wit as sparkling as her pendulous
diamond ear-rings. She flirted with all the men
outrageously.

Everyone seemed to be having a great time,
except Gina. She was still feeling uptight after her

set-to with Russell. Covertly she watched him, surprised at the way he tolerated Fiona's extrovert behaviour. He was not a tolerant individual, she would have thought, but he seemed not at all bothered that Fiona was playing to the gallery.

The band struck up again and Gina was pleased to find Peter Smythe asking her onto the floor. He at least was someone she always felt at home with. He was invariably good-humoured, a person with whom you could either be chatty or silent without any awkwardness.

When they returned to the table Russell and Fiona had moved on, but Mark was still enthusing about her. 'She's something else, isn't she? Pity she's tied up with that guy. Perhaps I should have rammed his molars down his throat!'

'Then you'd never have met the girl, idiot,' said Esther mildly.

Sitting between her and Gina, Chris put an arm around each of them. 'You can keep your Fiona . . . give me two nice hardworking nurses any time.'

'Thanks, Chris.' Gina gave a half-smile. 'I was beginning to feel redundant for a moment.'

It was twelve-thirty when the evening came to an end with the linking of hands in Auld Lang Syne. Afterwards people lingered over their goodbyes, finishing last drinks, reluctant to part company. Mark picked a carnation out of the flower arrangement and stuck it behind Gina's ear. 'Terrific evening, lover.'

'Yes, it was,' agreed Chris. Following Mark's example he placed a flower in Esther's hair and gallantly kissed her hand. 'We must all get together again some time. Can I give anyone a lift?'

'Well, all of us, actually,' put in Mark. 'We came by taxi. Come back to our place for coffee.'

After collecting their coats the girls made their way to the foyer. They found Chris and Mark waiting with Russell and Fiona. She was looking even more glamorous with a pale mink jacket over her sea-green dress.

'I was just saying it's much too early to break up the party,' Fiona announced blithely. 'Why don't we all wind up back at my flat?'

'Fine by me,' enthused Mark. 'Everyone agreed?'

Chris and Esther said they were game, but Gina hesitated. She had no wish to be thrust into close quarters with Russell and his society girlfriend. 'We—ell, would you mind if I don't? I'm on duty tomorrow and I'm useless if I don't get my eight hours. But you go, Mark,' she hastened to add as his face clouded.

He brightened. 'Sure you don't mind? We'll find someone going your way to give you a lift . . .'

Russell had made no comment until then, but now he cut in: 'No need to do that. I'll opt out too, if you can take Fiona. I'm on call tomorrow. I can drop Gina.'

'Oh, these workaholics!' deplored Fiona, but with Mark following in her wake like an eager bloodhound she didn't seem unduly disturbed that Russell was deserting her.

It was a worse situation than the one which Gina had wanted to avoid. While the others piled into

Chris's car and made for Knightsbridge, she found herself sitting alone alongside Russell in the dark green Jaguar.

'Would you have gone with them if I hadn't wanted to come home?' she ventured, hoping he didn't think she was a killjoy. 'I'd have been all right. You needn't have bothered.'

'It seems to be my role in life to get you safely home, doesn't it?' he returned with a meaning smile.

She ignored the innuendo and went on to say: 'It's my first day as sister tomorrow, otherwise I might have gone. I want to make a success of it.'

'That's as good an excuse as any.' Russell eased the car skilfully into the stream of traffic that hurtled from all directions.

'You don't need to worry about Mark and Fiona,' she said. 'He gets these enthusiasms, but he's quite harmless.'

He took the exit towards North London and the car purred ahead. 'I'm not worried about Fiona. She can take care of herself. She enjoys a change of audience.'

Gina stole a glance at him, his nonchalant expression puzzling her. Fiona was so attractive any man could be forgiven for having pangs of jealousy when she flirted with others. Yet here was Russell, apparently not giving a damn! Maybe in their strata of society it was considered sophisticated to be casual about personal relationships.

'And what about you?' he challenged, 'Are you scared that Fiona might seduce your friend Mark?'

'No!' She adopted his own air of indifference. 'He's not my property; he's a free agent.'

'So you're not breaking your heart?'

'Of course not. No strings . . . that's today's philosophy, isn't it?'

He suppressed a smile as he studied the road ahead. 'If you say so. I wouldn't know. I'm a mere beginner in these matters.'

'Such a beginner that you weren't slow to seize your opportunity last night!' she retorted sarcastically.

Russell laughed softly. 'Most men are opportunists you'll find, Gina. It's not every day one finds the glacier melting . . . but I sense the freeze has begun to set in again. Pity. I preferred last night's version.'

She let out a slow breath of exasperation. 'Has anyone ever told you how objectionable you are?'

'Actually, no. That's your considered opinion, is it?'

'Yes.'

They had reached her flat. He pulled up, switched off the engine and turned to look at her with narrowed eyes. 'So we have an original thinker here,' he taunted. 'I take it you don't need carrying in tonight?'

She refused to answer that. 'Thanks for the lift.' Coolly she released her seat-belt and felt for the door handle. He came round to her side of the car as she got out, walking with her to the porch and waiting while she put her key in the lock.

If he thought he was going to be invited in for coffee he was unlucky. 'Goodnight!' she said, turning briefly to face him before going in.

She was quite unprepared for what happened next. All at once she was in his arms and his mouth covered hers, possessive and compelling. For a moment she was overwhelmed, unable to resist the force of his will, then she pushed against him with fury, raising a hand to slap his face.

'Vixen!' he murmured, catching her wrist in an iron grasp. 'Is that the way for a lady to behave?'

Her breath came quickly. Eyes flashing, she glared at him. 'You . . . you . . .'

His face was barely inches from hers, his breath warm on her skin. 'I was merely returning the kiss you accused me of stealing last night,' he said with amused forbearance. 'You ought to say thank you.'

'Drop dead!' she flared.

'Say thank you,' he insisted.

'Let go, you beast. You're hurting my wrist.'

He loosened his grip without releasing her. 'I'm waiting!'

'Go to hell!'

'Well, in that case, I'll have it back again,' and with his free hand holding her head in a vice, he kissed her even more forcibly than before.

She *hated* him. And yet her body came alive at his touch. His lips became more tender and seeking, willing her to respond. Her pulses throbbed. For a moment she was in danger of weakening, then resolutely she pushed him away. Delivering a stinging slap to the side of his face, she slipped quickly into the house and slammed the door.

Holding flaming cheeks in her hands, Gina leaned against the closed door, panting. She heard his soft chuckle as he departed. She listened to the sound of the car engine purring to life and moving off before she went to her room.

Her limbs were trembling as she kicked off her shoes and started to undress. The barefaced audacity of the man! She was *glad* she had hit him, even though he was the senior medical registrar. He'd think twice about taking liberties with her in future, she thought defiantly.

Every word of their quarrel was vivid in her memory. *In that case I'll have it back again*, he'd said. Well, it showed a sense of humour, even if it was at her expense. Suddenly she found herself laughing, and then crying.

Gina slept well that night in spite of her turbulent emotions. It was past ten when she awoke the following morning. She hadn't to be on duty until midday, so she lay and brooded about the infuriating Russell Steele.

Last night *she* had won the battle, she decided, but in the cold light of day it was a hollow victory. She hated being on bad terms with anyone. There was more to it than that, though. She had this innate need to have him think well of her, and yet she had struck him; a thing she had never done to anyone else before. Now she thought they would always be at loggerheads. With all her heart she wished that it could have been otherwise.

If she had gone to the party at Fiona's with the rest then it wouldn't have happened. Gina hadn't heard the others come home and now she leapt out of bed, pulling on her dressing-gown, to see if Esther was awake and to find out how they had fared.

To her surprise her flatmate's room was empty, the bed unslept in. Puzzled, Gina went to the kitchen to make herself a drink. It was Esther's day off, so perhaps Chris had taken her straight home.

It occurred to her to see if Mark was around, but upstairs she found no sign of him either. She began to imagine all sorts of things . . . road accidents and the like. Then her mind was put at rest by the sound of the front door opening and cheerful voices on the doorstep.

Racing downstairs again she found Esther and Mark waving goodbye to Chris as he drove off.

'So there you are. Where've you been?' demanded Gina.

'Oh, you should have come with us,' Esther said, looking bouncy if a bit crumpled. 'Fiona's got the most gorgeous flat. *Daddy* bought it for her. They must be rolling in it.'

'You stayed there all night?'

'Mmm!' Mark yawned and combed his fingers through his untidy sandy hair. 'We kipped down on her shag-pile. We'd all had a bit too much bubbly to take to the road. She cooked us egg and bacon before kicking us out this morning. What a girl!' His expression was one of total bliss. 'How that guy Russell keeps up with her I don't know. I'm whacked. G'night girls!' and he ambled off up to his own room.

Esther followed Gina into the kitchen and flopped on a chair. 'How the other half of the world lives!' she sighed. 'I don't think Chris was over-impressed actually. He's quite a puritan at heart, isn't he?'

'D'you think so?' Gina smiled to herself as she made coffee for her friend. 'I wouldn't have called him that in the old days.'

'Oh, not puritanical in *that* sense. I mean, he just thinks wealth should be shared around more evenly.'

Gina eyed her flatmate askance. 'Sounds like you got into some weighty discussions?'

'Yes, I suppose we did. He's interesting. Nice too. He's coming round later today. There's a book he's promised to lend me.'

'Oh, pity I shan't be around,' said Gina with a grin. 'You'll have to entertain him all on your own.'

'How did you make out with Russell last night?'

'We just came straight home and parted on the doorstep,' Gina returned casually. She did not want to talk about last night, even to Esther.

Back in her room, dressing in her new blue uniform ready for work, she was hopeful that things might possibly work out between Esther and Chris. The ball appeared to have been a success for them even if it had been a disaster for herself. But right now there were more important issues to think about than the outrageous Russell Steele. She had a new job to do and she was going to do it well. He would not be able to fault her on that score.

CHAPTER SEVEN

Winter came down hard at the beginning of December. Most of the country was wrapped in ice and snow and the weather brought its usual toll of health problems.

There were no spare beds on Harvey Ward during Gina's initial period as Sister, and she found herself constantly waylaid by anxious visitors wanting information about patients. It was not always easy to judge whether people wished to hear the truth or merely to be reassured. And whereas some were full of gratitude for all that was being done for their relatives, in others fear of the unknown could make them quite belligerent. All had to be dealt with as considerately as possible.

But Gina was glad to be busy. It gave her less time to worry about family and personal problems. Contrary to expectations, since Jason's departure for Paris she had seen less of Mark than usual. And since the night of the ball he had been more chirpy than ever. It took no great stretch of the imagination to see that it had something to do with Fiona. Gina had heard them on the phone one evening and drawn her own conclusions.

Esther also was in good spirits, having had several dates with Chris since the ball. Whether anything permanent would come of it still remained to be seen, but at least it was helping her to forget her previous unsatisfactory love affair.

During the second week of December Gina's father returned from his tour of the Far East. They were reunited over dinner at a West End hotel one evening. She found him looking tanned and prosperous. Nevertheless, when talking about the family, Gina detected the self-doubt behind the successful businessman.

'What's my grandson like?' he wanted to know as they sat over coffee after their meal.

'Gorgeous, Dad. When are you going down?'

'We—ell, I thought maybe at the weekend. Can you come too?'

'Sorry, I'm working. Mummy's there.'

He lit up a cigar and let out a stream of aromatic smoke. 'Yes, I know. We spoke on the phone. It might be a bit . . . awkward. I'm in the dog-house, I suppose you know?' he said somewhat self-consciously.

'You probably asked for it,' said Gina with a half-smile. 'Come on, Dad, why don't *you* make the grand gesture. Mummy only needs to feel, well . . . wanted.'

'Don't we all?' he returned.

She searched in her handbag for a tissue as emotion clouded her eyes, and she came across his ticket for the carol concert. 'Oh, look!' she exclaimed brightly, passing it to him, 'You're back in time for this. I hoped you would be.'

He studied it with interest. 'This Thursday. Yes, I think I can make that. I enjoyed it last year.'

'Good. See you there, then. Wait for me in the foyer afterwards and we'll have a drink together.'

She said nothing about having posted a ticket to her mother. They would be sitting together, all being well, which was about as far as Gina could go to help their reconciliation.

On the day before the actual event there was a final practice for the carol concert in the Royal Festival Hall itself. With several hundred people in the combined hospital choirs it needed careful organisation to get everyone properly seated on the platform. The celebrity conductor co-opted for the occasion put them through their paces. He stamped his own genial zest on the assembly, uniting the groups into one harmonious whole.

At the end of the rehearsal Gina had to dash away to Waterloo station, where she had arranged to meet her mother. She was glad of the excuse not to join the others for the usual social drink. Following her flare-up with Russell after the ball she thought it best to avoid his company off the ward. It was quite hard enough having to meet him during the course of their work.

She reached the station with only minutes to spare. The train drew in and Laura Brent, looking trim and attractive in her camel-hair travel coat, angora scarf and hat, stepped lightly down the platform amid the general exodus.

Waiting by the barrier, Gina waved vigorously, and the two were soon greeting each other with a warm hug and kiss.

Chatting non-stop they made for the Underground. Yes, the baby was fine, Melly was a born mother and John was becoming quite adept at nappy-changing. 'I feel superfluous most of the time,' said Gina's mother, laughing, 'but I shall stay on there until the New Year. Then I shall have to decide what I'm going to do with myself.'

'Won't you go back to the Kensington flat?'

Laura Brent shrugged. 'I haven't thought that far ahead yet. What are you going to do tomorrow, Gina?'

'I'm working until four-thirty, I'm afraid.'

'Okay, I'll slip up to Oxford Street and do some shopping. Then I'll have a meal out and come straight on to the concert. That will be best I think, because you'll probably need to get there earlier, won't you?'

'Yes, we have to get changed, and it'll be a mad scramble behind the scenes.'

Esther followed them in soon after they reached the house and they sat down to coffee together. Mark also was called down to be introduced.

'And are you coming to this concert?' Gina's mother asked him.

'Not my scene,' grinned Mark. 'In any case I'm dashing home tomorrow to collect my ski-ing gear. I've been invited to a Christmas house party in Gstaad.'

The girls both looked at him in surprise. 'That's a turn-up, isn't it?' said Esther. 'Mixing with the rich and famous, are we?'

'I'm just making the number up, but it could be interesting.' He drank his coffee without being more forthcoming.

Dressed ready for work the following morning Gina took her mother a cup of tea in bed.

'Fancy you, a Sister!' Laura Brent said, admiring

her daughter in her neat dark blue uniform. 'I can
hardly believe it. Doesn't seem all that long ago
when we left you with your suitcase like a poor little
orphan at the Nurses' Home. And now here you
are in charge of a ward. You've never regretted
choosing nursing instead of music?'

'No,' said Gina. 'I still love music, of course, but
I don't think I'd have been good enough to make
a career of it . . . I mean, not to have got to the
top.'

She found herself thinking of the concert that
Russell had taken her to, and there he was back in
her mind. Well, at least music was something they
didn't fall out about. For him, as for her, it was one
of the bright strands of life that lifted it above the
commonplace.

With an effort she brought herself back to the
present. 'Well, I'll have to be moving. I'll look out
for you tonight, Mummy. Esther and I are quite
near the front of the stage. See you later, darling.'

In the forecourt of St Benedict's the two great
evergreens had been hung with fairy-lights as a
customary part of the Christmas decorations. Garlands were already brightening the rather shabby
green paintwork in the entrance hall. Individual
wards were not allowed to decorate until much
nearer Christmas, unnecessary hangings being considered a fire risk, but each ward had its own fund
with which to buy a few festive touches.

Taking the night report from Molly Stevens,
Gina learned that there had been an overnight
admission.

'Mr Colby, aged forty-three, came up at mid-night from Casualty. Peptic ulcer,' Molly read from her notes. 'He collapsed at work, haemoglobin six on admission. He's on intravenous whole-blood, AB positive. We've just put up the last pack so you'll need to send down to the Path Lab for some more. Nil by mouth because they'll be doing a gastroscopy sometime soon.'

With the report concluded, the day staff went about their tasks of washings and bed-making before breakfasts were served. Gina, meanwhile, made her customary tour of the ward, starting with the new patient, Mr Colby. She found a well-built man but with a tell-tale pallor underlying a day's growth of beard. 'I feel a mess,' he said, passing a limp hand over his stubble. 'The wife's going to bring my shaving kit in later.'

'I'll get one of the nurses to find you a razor for the time being,' promised Gina. 'You'll feel much better for a shave, won't you?'

There had been a change round of some of the student nurses on the wards and Gina was not sorry that Sharon Evans had now moved on. Her place had been taken by Mimi Tong, a gentle dark-eyed girl from Thailand. Her command of English was good, except that she muddled her r's and l's in an endearing sort of way. She was eager to learn, had a nice way with the patients, and Gina felt she was going to be an asset to the department.

'Mimi, I think you could write up Mr Colby for your case history,' Gina said when breakfasts were cleared away and the morning routines attended to. 'He seems to be a co-operative man, so you should have no difficulty. You know all the questions to ask, don't you?'

'Yes, Sister, we did that in our rast study brock.'

'Right, and include any personal observations which you think it might help us to know.'

Armed with her notepad and ballpoint, Mimi trotted off eagerly, dark hair swinging, to sit beside Mr Colby and learn about the circumstances that had led up to his collapse.

Settling down to her administrative work, Gina tied up the latest Path Lab reports with individual case notes and telephoned the medical social worker about a patient who was worried about his financial affairs. She arranged for the ECG technician to visit and made out the drugs order for the Dispensary. There was also the Maintenance Dept to be contacted about a fused light in the ward.

Mid-morning drinks were being served to the patients when Peter Smythe and the registrar arrived to see Mr Colby.

'Your colour's improving, sir. How are you feeling now?' Russell enquired, checking the patient's pulse.

'Not a great deal better,' admitted Mr Colby wearily. 'Still got this pain in my gut, I'm afraid.'

'Well, you will have for a while.' Russell turned to his houseman. 'We'd better have another haemoglobin count. Will you see to that?'

Peter nodded and went off to collect the necessary equipment for the blood test.

Back in the office Russell sat down at Gina's desk and wrote up the case notes. It was the first time she had been alone with him since slapping his face after the ball. He darted her a glance from under his dark brows as he wrote.

'And where did you shoot off to after the rehearsal last night?'

'I went to meet my mother, if it's any concern of yours.'

'Don't be waspish. Paul Waring will probably be up later to see Mr Colby about the gastroscopy.'

'I supposed he would be.'

'Have you talked to him since your, er . . . misadventure?'

'No, I haven't. Perhaps he's keeping out of my way.'

'Wise guy. For a featherweight you pack quite a punch. Perhaps I should warn him what a spitfire you are.'

Her cheeks grew pink, but she faced him squarely as he put his pen in his coat pocket and rose to go. 'You asked for what you got. Nothing Paul gets up to surprises me, but I expected better of you.'

'A sting in the tongue as well?' he taunted. 'Don't put people on pedestals, Gina.' He paused as he was about to leave. 'By the way, I want you to do me a small favour.'

His expression was matter-of-fact, not frivolous, but she eyed him warily. 'What's that?'

'Orthopaedics can now take that chappie with the slipped disc off your hands. You can transfer him as soon as you like. So you'll have an empty bed, won't you?'

'And who do you want us to take?'

He looked half-apologetic. 'There's an old fellow down in Casualty. He's not clinically ill, apart from malnutrition and self-neglect. I know Harvey is acute medical but I don't want to put him with the chronics. He needs cheering up and feeding up. No living relatives as far as I can tell.'

'Yes, of course we'll take him.'

'Thank you.'

Reluctantly admiring his powerful frame as he strode away, Gina was thoughtful. She suspected that Russell Steele had a soft centre beneath his tough exterior, although he would probably rather die than have it known. But that was men all over, wasn't it? she mused. To admit to being tender-hearted might ruin their image. Her father was much the same. And he certainly never found it easy to admit to being wrong. Gina sighed and hoped she was doing the right thing in bringing her parents together at the carol concert. Turning her thoughts to work again she set about making arrangements for the transfer of the orthopaedic patient.

It was after lunch before a staff nurse from Casualty brought up the old man Russell had spoken about. She handed the notes to Gina in the office. 'His name's Reuben Chambers. He's seventy-five. We've given him a bath and he smells a bit sweeter now. Don't think he could have been near water for about a month,' she chuckled.

Through the window Gina glanced at the white-haired emaciated pensioner in the wheelchair, heightened spots of colour on his prominent cheekbones. 'Poor old chap,' she said, 'he must have felt pretty low to let himself get into that state.'

She detailed Lynn Davis to see him into bed and

make out his charts and later, when she had a moment to spare, Gina went over to introduce herself. 'Hallo, Mr Chambers, I'm Sister Brent. Are you beginning to feel a little better?'

'Yes, thank you, my dear. I'm afraid I've been rather a nuisance to everyone. I'm sorry.' His old blue eyes looked regretful. He was very polite and well-spoken and had obviously seen better days.

'Don't worry about it!' Gina said, smiling. 'Doctor wants us to feed you up a bit, but you must try and take care of yourself once we get you fit again. Don't you have meals-on-wheels at home?'

'Good gracious, no. I've always managed for myself. But I haven't been feeling so good for the past few weeks . . . rheumatism in my knees and a bit of a cold . . . things just got beyond me for a while.'

'Isn't there someone we can contact for you?' She felt he would need keeping an eye on when he did go home.

The old man shook his head. 'My wife died twenty years ago. We were both only children. We did have a daughter, but she was retarded and she's gone now. No, there's no-one to tell.'

'What about your neighbours?'

'I don't see much of them, they're out at work all day.'

It was a sad but familiar story. Gina knew only too well that there were many such lonely old people around. This man was proud and independent and they would need to be diplomatic in trying to get him help when he was discharged. In the meantime she hoped it would be possible to keep him in over Christmas so that at least he would have warmth and companionship during the holiday.

The afternoon was a busy one with visits from a number of consultants. As expected, Paul Waring arrived to see Mr Colby about his gastroscopy. At the time, however, Gina was with a visiting neurologist, so that she was glad not to have to bother with Paul. He probably had a guilty conscience anyway about lacing her drinks, she decided, so it would do him good to live with it a bit longer. When four-thirty came she was glad to be able to hand over and get off to prepare for the concert that evening.

Back at the house she and Esther had a snack together before getting themselves ready.

'Mum phoned me this morning to say my father can't make it,' Esther mentioned, 'so I rang Chris and he's coming instead. He's meeting my mother there. Hope they find each other.'

'They've met before, have they?' asked Gina.

'Yes, he came in for coffee when he took me home the other night.'

So it hadn't taken long for Chris to be taken home to meet the family, thought Gina with a private smile. 'We'd better get a move on,' she said, looking at the clock as she finished her sandwich, 'or they'll be there and we won't.'

Presently, with freshly-laundered uniforms in their holdalls, they made for the Underground and Waterloo Station, walking the short distance from there to the Royal Festival Hall. The reception area of the brightly lit concert hall was already thronging with people. Early visitors were meeting friends

while performers made their way backstage to get
ready.

Behind the scenes there was good-natured jost-
ling in the crowded changing rooms. Gina and
Esther found themselves a space, wriggled out of
jeans and sweaters and put on their uniforms,
exchanging lively greetings with people they recognised.

Sally Yates waved energetically from the crowd
assembling in the wings when the girls finally
emerged to take their places in the correct line-up.
She was standing with Peter and Russell, both
looking debonair in black dinner jackets.

'Come on, you two, we thought you'd got lost!'
breezed Peter, making room for them in front of
him.

'We very nearly got trampled to death back
there,' Esther grinned. 'Lord knows if we'll ever
find our things again.'

'I know. Pandemonium, isn't it?' Sally agreed,
'But what can you expect with a crowd like this?'

'You should come ready dressed, like we do,' put
in Russell. His dark eyes deliberately sought
Gina's.

'It's all very well for you,' she retorted, looking
him over, 'but you don't have to live in uniform.
Personally I'm glad to get out of it.'

A flourish of music from the massive organ
diverted everyone's attention. The waiting corps of
military trumpeters, resplendent in dress uniform,
began to take their places on the topmost tier at the
back of the stage.

'This is it!' said Peter, and the singers began to

file to their prearranged positions.

The nurses in the foremost row each carried a lighted lantern, lending a Christmas card touch to the occasion. Banked behind them rose the tiers of other hospital staffs, the women's colourful stripes and pastels, snowy aprons and caps contrasting with the sober-suited men.

From their places on the stage Gina and Esther scanned the vast, expectant audience. A discreetly waving hand caught Gina's eye and spotting her parents sitting together she smiled in their direction. Esther, too, had seen her mother and Chris and relaxed now that she knew they were there.

Waiting for the performance to begin, Gina was acutely conscious of Russell's presence in the row immediately behind her. She sensed that his eyes were upon her and it was all she could do to resist the urge to turn round. He and Peter began to talk quietly together. 'What happened to Paul Waring?' she heard Russell enquire, 'I don't see him in the tenors.'

'No, he had to drop out,' Peter murmured. 'He's operating tonight, anyway.'

A burst of applause signalled the arrival of the conductor to his rostrum. A hush fell over the company. The lights dimmed. The bandsmen raised their shining trumpets and with a resounding fanfare the programme began.

For Gina it was the remembered moving experience. The richness of massed voices backed by swelling organ music, stirring trumpets, clashing cymbals and drums. Only this time it was coupled with the distinctive sound of Russell's vibrant tones in the tier behind. If he hadn't chosen to be a doctor he could have succeeded equally well as a singer, she thought. It was uncanny, the effect a human voice could have on one.

The introductory carol was a familiar one in which the audience was invited to join and did so wholeheartedly. There followed a varied programme by the choir, lesser known but enchanting carols from other lands alternating with more old favourites.

Under the benevolent influence of the conductor *The Twelve Days of Christmas* was sung by all. He divided up the auditorium, summoning each section to come in with its appropriate line, a performance which ended in some confusion and much hilarity.

Towards the end Gina's own favourite *Ring Out, Wild Bells* brought the lump to her throat as usual, and finally the concert came to its memorable climax with a riotous rendering of *We wish you a Merry Christmas*.

With applause still ringing in their ears the company filed off stage. All were eager to meet up with friends and relatives afterwards. In the general scramble towards the dressing rooms Gina and Esther lost sight of the rest of their group. Unearthing their belongings they found a corner in which to change before joining the milling crowds on the staircases.

Over the banister Esther saw her mother and Chris in the distance. 'See you later,' she said to Gina as she ran off to join them.

On the first-floor level Gina found her own

parents standing together waiting for her, both apparently in a congenial frame of mind. 'Hi!' she exclaimed cheerfully, hurrying up to them, 'Did you enjoy it?'

'Yes, splendid show!' her father enthused. 'Would you like a drink now?'

'Please. A lager and lime. I'm gasping.'

'Right, you two find a table and I'll get them.'

He disappeared in the direction of the bar and Laura Brent wagged a finger at her daughter. 'You didn't say your father was going to be here,' she accused.

Gina grinned. 'Well, I'd bought the two tickets and Dad was back, so why not?' There were no spare seats so they stood around. 'I thought you were going shopping today. No parcels?'

Her mother gave a quiet smile. 'Yes, I did well, but I didn't want to lug them here so I left them at Kensington since I had my key with me. Your father was there,' she added.

'Oh,' said Gina, 'so you came together?'

'Yes. We had a talk. He's coming back to Melly's with me tomorrow, to see the baby.'

Mr Brent was not alone when he returned with their drinks. With him was a distinguished silver-haired man of guardslike stature. 'Laura, you remember Sir Richard, don't you? We met in the States a couple of years ago.'

'Yes, of course,' said Gina's mother with a gracious smile. 'How is your wife?'

'She's well, thank you,' said Sir Richard, shaking her by the hand in a courtly fashion. 'I've sent my son to bring her over. Ah, here they are now,' he went on as Russell arrived accompanied by his mother. There were introductions all round.

'Gina and I have met already,' Lady Steele said, smiling. 'We spent a very pleasant evening together recently. Strange, isn't it, that our children should be working at the same hospital?'

There followed mutual praise for the excellence of the carol concert before the parents began reminiscing about their American trip. It left Gina with no alternative but to talk to Russell as though they were the best of friends.

'So it's peace on earth and goodwill to registrars?' he murmured, his dark eyes provocative.

'Of course,' she returned sweetly, determined to keep calm despite the upheaval he always managed to create inside her. 'I'm filled with charity tonight.'

'A case of music charms the savage breast?'

'Something like that, I suppose.'

'A pity we can't make it a permanent state of affairs.'

'Yes, isn't it? But then life's not one long musical comedy, sadly.'

He chuckled, treating her to a steady, discerning scrutiny. 'On the contrary, there is a certain similarity at times, at least where you're concerned.'

Gina finished her drink and put the glass on a table. 'I promised to look out for Esther,' she said, seeing that the foyer was beginning to empty of people.

'And we must be going,' put in Sir Richard.

The two families exchanged seasonal greetings and parted company. Gina's father went off to collect his overcoat from the cloakroom.

'Are you coming back with me, Mum?' Gina asked as they stood waiting for him.

'Well, as I've got to go back to Kensington to pick up my shopping I may as well spend the night there,' said Laura Brent, buttoning up her coat and putting on her gloves, 'then your father and I can drive straight back to Lyndhurst tomorrow. You don't mind, do you dear?'

'Of course not,' Gina said cheerfully, and after seeing her parents on their way she went in search of her flatmate.

Esther, with her mother and Chris, was also on the point of leaving. 'Oh, there you are!' she said, 'Have your folks gone?'

'Yes, are you coming home now?'

'We're taking Mummy back first. Chris has got his car here. Come with us?'

Gina was on the point of accepting but on second thoughts decided not to. 'Well, thanks all the same, but I think I'll go straight back. It doesn't take long on the train. See you later.'

Waving them goodbye, she turned up her coat collar and joined the people making for the Underground. She felt a little abandoned, going home on her own after the companionship of the evening, but it was her own choice, wanting to give Chris and Esther time to themselves. It was a bitterly cold night and she had lost her gloves. Her free hand she put in her pocket but she needed the other to carry her bag and her fingers were soon chilled.

Walking briskly with the crowd, she was suddenly surprised to find Russell falling into step beside her. 'Hallo!' he said, affably, 'Going home?'

'Hallo!' she returned. The glow of the music was still with her and she felt pleased to have his company. 'Yes, I'm on my way to the station. Esther's seeing her mother home first.'

'I've got my car here, I'll give you a lift. Let me take that for you.' He relieved her of the holdall, touching her hand in the process. 'My goodness, your fingers are frozen. No gloves?'

She shook her head ruefully. 'I started out with some. They got lost in the crush backstage.'

His own hands, although bare, were warm as toast, and grasping hers he plunged it into his overcoat pocket and held it there; a situation which she found both comforting and disquieting. She had to quicken her pace to keep up with his long stride.

'I'm afraid I'm using the same grotty garage that I was in last time we were here together, remember?'

'Don't remind me!' she said with a slight shudder. 'It's not an experience I'd like to repeat!' The whole nightmarish episode came back to her . . . the shots in the dark archway, the blood-soaked victim, her dash to the phone. That was the first time Russell had kissed her.

He smiled down at her reassuringly and squeezed the hand he held in his pocket. 'Don't worry. It's not likely to happen again.'

This time they reached the car park without incident. Soon they were out of the dark back streets and into brightly lit thoroughfares where shop windows glittered with the trappings of commercial Christmas.

In a smart salon window Gina glimpsed an exotic

model ballgown in scarlet. It reminded her of someone. 'No Fiona tonight?' she asked conversa-
tionally.

'No. Actually Fiona went off to Gstaad this
morning, for the winter sports.'

'Oh!' said Gina, her mind leaping back to last
night in the flat. Gstaad! That was the place Mark
had mentioned in connection with the house party
he'd been invited to. Was that coincidence or de-
sign? She decided it was best not to comment. 'Will
you be joining her?' she asked.

'No, I don't ski. And what are you doing for the
holiday?'

'Working. I'm having New Year off instead.'

'So we'll be holding the fort together,' he remarked with a sideways smile that made her heart
leap. 'Since Christmas is for the kids I supposed I
ought to let the family guys have the time off.'

'Noble of you,' she said.

'Isn't it? Inside every sinner there's a saint waiting to get out!'

She stole a glance at his strong profile. He was
intent on negotiating the traffic, but his expression
was warm and friendly, and he was poking fun at
himself, not at her. He really did seem to be going
out of his way to be agreeable for a change. She
almost wished he would revert to being his usual
infuriating self, which would at least give her a
reason for disliking him. If he continued to be
charming and considerate she wouldn't be able to
stop herself from loving him, Fiona or no Fiona.
And that would be no recipe for her future happiness because he had made it plain when he had

taken her to the Mendelssohn concert that he had
no interest in her from a personal point of view.

True, he had kissed her on three occasions now;
once out of compassion and twice out of devilment.
She wondered how they would part tonight. A
shiver of anticipation ran through her at the prospect of what might be looming. Suppose he were
tempted to play the fool again, to try his luck? Her
inclination at that moment was to be submissive, to
enjoy every moment of his undeniable appeal.
Common sense warned her to be prudent. Even if
he did attempt to flirt with her it would only be
another display of opportunism, as he had pointed
out once before.

But she need have had no fears. When he drew
up outside the flat, his parting was brief to the point
of terseness. 'Well, thanks for your company.
Goodnight,' and he drove away immediately.

With a perverse feeling of disappointment Gina
let herself into the empty house. She made herself a
nightcap and carried it through to her room, brooding on the complexities of life. She was aware of a
subtle change in the situation between herself and
Russell, although exactly what or why she couldn't
fathom. Tonight he had not resorted to his old
peremptory manner towards her, but neither had
he become any more approachable. Indeed, when
he had said goodbye one would have thought he
couldn't wait to get rid of her. It was almost as
though he were afraid of her. That was a ridiculous
notion, but there was something in the air she could
not put her finger on.

Gina sat in front of the mirror removing her eye

make-up, and a disconsolate face stared back at her. She wished with all her heart she could put the clock back and start on a better footing with Russell. Even if there could never be anything between them it would at least be something to have him perpetually agreeable. Except, of course, he would have her completely crazy about him in that case. One way or the other she was bound to be a loser.

Oh, what the hell, she thought with a careless shrug, he can take a running jump for all I care. But for all her bravado, deep down she knew she was kidding herself and the elation of the evening crumbled into dust.

CHAPTER EIGHT

RUSSELL continued to haunt Gina's thoughts long after she had gone to bed that night. Even with his physical presence removed she could feel the subtle draw of his influence. As though, in some strange way, he had the power to direct her mind.

She relived their journey home together, trying to be heartened by the signs of a thaw in his manner. Even if it meant nothing more than respect for her as a colleague, at least it showed that she was not entirely beneath his notice. Perhaps it was a good thing that the hospital world was a transitory one. She would not be staying at St Benedict's for ever. When she moved on she would be able to get him out of her hair.

It was into the small hours before she finally fell asleep after making a determined effort to dismiss him from her mind, awaking the following morning to the sounds of Esther moving about in the bathroom. For a while she lay in a state of limbo until a carol tune running through her head brought Russell and the previous night vividly to the fore.

Thoroughly impatient with herself, she leapt out of bed, pulled on her dressing-gown and made her way to the kitchen where she lighted the gas oven to warm the room. Switching on the radio she caught the weather forecast: 'Heavy snowfalls are causing chaos on motorways in the North' came the reader's voice. Glancing at the leaden sky through the window Gina guessed that it wouldn't be too long before the same kind of weather arrived in London.

Collecting the milk from the doorstep, she also picked up the morning delivery of post, mainly Christmas cards, and after making two mugs of coffee she sat down to sort through them.

Esther joined her, looking pink and scrubbed and exuberant, her dark hair pulled back into a damp pony-tail.

Gina pushed over her friend's share of the mail. 'You're looking pleased with life,' she said.

'Well, it *was* rather a nice end to the evening,' returned Esther with a faraway smile.

'What did you do? I didn't hear you come home.'

'It was after two. We dropped my mother off and then went back to Chris's place for a while.'

'You two seem to be hitting it off rather well. On the same wavelength, are you?'

'Mmm, you could say that,' admitted Esther contentedly. 'You don't mind, do you?' she added with a quick glance at Gina.

'Mind? Good heavens, no! I'm glad if you're glad. At least that's one of us on the up-and-up for the moment. By the way,' Gina went on, 'you know Mark's going to this house party in Gstaad? Well, I've discovered that Fiona is out there too.'

Esther gave a low whistle. 'Wow! Is that a coincidence or isn't it? He was being a bit cagey I thought. How did you find out?'

'Russell told me. He's not going himself, so I didn't mention about Mark. Not that he seemed bothered about her taking off without him. I can't make out that couple. He goes his way and she goes hers.'

'Oh well, it takes all sorts,' said Esther. From the dreamy look in her eyes it was clear she had only one couple on her mind at that moment—herself and Chris.

'When are you seeing him again?' Gina prompted.

'Chris? Actually not until Boxing Day. Mum invited him to our place for Christmas lunch but he'd already promised to go home. You'll be here on your own, won't you? Come on to us after you leave work?'

'I'll be all right,' said Gina. 'There'll be a party in the doctors' mess, and I'll be going home for New Year, so I'll save my celebrations for then. Thanks all the same.'

Going on duty at midday, Gina took the report from her staff nurse and caught up with events on the ward. Ben, the diabetic boy, was for discharge and arrangements were being made for outpatient counselling sessions to help him come to terms with his problems. The gastroscopy on Mr Colby had confirmed the peptic ulcer and it was hoped to clear it up with drugs and diet. Old Reuben Chambers was on a course of an anti-inflammatory drug to help his aches and pains.

When the ward post came up Gina distributed it herself and had a cheerful word with the patients. Coming to Mr Colby she was surprised to find him looking depressed in spite of his satisfactory progress report. He was off the blood transfusion although still on a dextrose drip, and his bed had been moved further down the ward since he did not need to be under such close surveillance.

'How's the tummy now, Mr Colby?' she asked. 'Any more pain?'

'No, Sister. I'm fine,' he said, making an effort to be bright. 'Dr Steele says I'm to have a barium meal after Christmas to check how things are going.'

Gina smiled reassuringly. 'It only means sipping a thick sort of drink so that the X-ray can pick up any trouble spots. Not worried about it, are you?'

'No, I'm not worried about that. I'm a bit bothered about my wife, though. I mean, she hasn't been too well herself, long before I got sick. I've told her and told her to go to the quack, but she won't. I know what it is,' he went on, frowning, 'she's afraid she's got a growth. She's put on a lot of weight since she had the change, and she gets shocking indigestion. I—I wondered if you could have a word with her, Sister . . . tell her she ought to see someone?'

'We—ell,' said Gina hesitantly, 'I would like to help, but she might resent my interfering, or the fact that you'd talked to me about it. It's rather difficult.' She patted his hand. 'Maybe the chance will present itself . . . we'll have to play it by ear. Try not to worry.'

The afternoon visitors were waiting outside the ward at the conclusion of the drugs round and Mimi opened the doors to let them in. Sitting at her desk Gina watched the trickle of people making their way past the beds. She caught Mrs Colby's eye and smiled warmly as the woman made her rather lumbering progress to see her husband.

Mrs Colby was a middle-aged woman with fading brown curly hair, but there was still a certain prettiness about her plump face. She was obviously carrying to much weight under her loose coat. Her ankles looked puffy, but her features were not drawn, neither was there that yellowish tinge about her skin that could sometimes be associated with cancer sufferers. In fact her complexion had a healthy glow. Maybe she had been eating for comfort and putting on weight that way. And her indigestion could be dietary.

Certainly getting into a state over his wife's health was not going to help Mr Colby's ulcer, but Gina didn't see what she could do unless the woman approached her voluntarily. You couldn't thrust advice at people uninvited.

Gina turned her mind to more immediate matters. There was less than a week now to Christmas and she called the staff into the office to discuss ideas for decorating the ward.

'The Ward Fund is quite healthy,' she said. 'I've seen some large cut-outs in Hardwicks—Santa Claus shooting over the roofs in a space ship. We could stick some of those on the walls.'

'And we can have the usual cottonwool snow at the windows and tinsel along the curtain rails,' Lynn Davis put in. 'We've got a fantastic holly bush in the garden at the back of my digs. It's covered in berries, so I'll bring in a bunch of that. Men don't get many flowers, do they?'

'We could have a rittle artificial Chlistmas tlee for the table,' suggested Mimi.

'Okay, I'll leave that to you then,' smiled Gina. She pointed to a large carton on the floor. 'The Rotary Club have sent us up some hanging decorations and a number of small presents so that everyone will have something on their breakfast tray on Christmas morning.' They all began to feel quite festive, especially when Mimi came back from answering a bell, bringing with her a large box of chocolates. 'Mr Mollis's wife says these are for us.'

'Better start watching your waistlines, girls!' warned Gina, stripping off the cellophane and leaving the box open on the desk for all to help themselves.

Father Donoghue, the hospital chaplain, popped his head around the door, his lean face wreathed in smiles. 'Good afternoon all,' he said.

'Hallo, Father, help yourself to a choc,' Gina invited.

'Thank you.' He studied the contents list carefully before selecting a sweet. 'I'll be holding communion on Christmas morning. Any new patients you think would like to see me now?'

Gina glanced across at old Reuben, sitting in a chair by his bed in a hospital dressing-gown. He had no visitors, nor was likely to have. She nodded in his direction. 'There's Mr Chambers over there. His milkman discovered him in a state of collapse. He lives alone and doesn't have any relatives. It says C of E on his notes. He might welcome a chat.'

'Right, I'll go and see him.' The minister ambled off and was soon in conversation with the old man. Gina knew he was not the sort to push religion down people's throats; he was a pleasantly chatty soul, letting people unburden themselves if they wished to or moving on if his presence was not welcomed. But Reuben seemed only too happy to put down his newspaper and talk.

The staff dispersed to their various tasks. On her way out a visitor stopped by the office with a bunch of golden incurved chrysanthemums. 'My husband doesn't want these on his locker; he says they'll be better in the middle of the ward where everyone can see them,' she explained.

'Oh, thank you. They're beautiful,' said Gina. 'I'll find a vase.'

She took the flowers along to the ward kitchen and was reaching up to a shelf for a suitable container when two hands gripped her round the waist. She jumped and turned to find Paul Waring grinning at her.

'What do *you* want?' she said, pushing his hands away.

'That's no way to greet your number-one fan.' His small eyes gleamed wickedly. 'How did you make out that night?'

'Which night?' she countered, giving him a long, straight look.

'The last time we were together, sweetheart. In the doctors' mess, don't you remember? Phipps' and Andrea's drinks do.'

'Oh, *that* night. Fine. Why?' she returned carelessly.

He looked a little nonplussed. 'Nothing . . . I just wondered . . .'

'All right, Paul,' cut in Gina with a wry grin. 'Don't think I didn't know what you were up to.

I've warned all the girls to keep their hands over their glasses when you're about.'

He put on a contrite face, produced a sprig of mistletoe and held it over her head. 'Forgiven, am I? Kiss and make up?'

'Well, as it's Christmas,' and she allowed him to kiss her. She laughed as she finally wriggled out of his grasp. 'What did you come for? Not just for that, was it?'

'Steele wants me to see one of his patients about a bronchoscopy . . .'

Only then did Gina catch sight of Russell Steele himself standing in the doorway, his face unsmiling. 'Sorry to interrupt,' he said tartly, 'but could we get on with it?'

Her cheeks flamed and her stomach lurched. How long had he been there? she wondered. And it suddenly mattered very much that he shouldn't think badly of her, but to attempt explanations would only be regarded as a sign of guilt. She squared her shoulders and stared back at him equally coolly. 'You're speaking of Mr Morgan, I presume? It is time for the visitors to leave,' she went on, glancing at her watch, 'so go ahead.'

Russell left them and strode down the ward, white coat flapping.

Paul made a dubious face at her. 'Ouch! What's biting him? Think we may both have been black-listed. *C'est la vie!*' He sauntered out to join the registrar at Mr Morgan's bedside.

Once again Gina felt like slaughtering Paul Waring. She should have known better than to have let him come within an inch of her. To com-

pose herself she spent a little time arranging the
flowers before marching down the ward, head high,
to place them on the central table.

'Sister!' Russell beckoned her over to where Paul
was in process of having Mr Morgan sign the consent form for an anaesthetic. 'Nothing more by
mouth for Mr Morgan. He's going to have his
bronchoscopy later tonight.'

Paul gave her a stealthy wink as he wrote the
required pre-med onto the patient's headboard and
handed it to her. 'I'll give you a ring when I'm
ready, but it won't be before ten o'clock. See you
later, sir,' he said blithely to Mr Morgan.

The two doctors walked away discussing the
case, leaving Gina to straighten the bed curtains
and rearrange the patient's pillows.

'Is that comfortable?' she asked as Mr Morgan
lay back, puffing a little after his exertions.

'Yes, thank you, love. Glad they're going to put
me out for this business. Can't be funny, having a
tube stuck down your throat.'

'The injection you have before you go down will
make you feel nice and sleepy. You won't know
much about it after that. You'll have a bit of a sore
throat when you wake up, that's all. And the
sooner it's done, the better.'

'If you say so. You'll be off-duty when I go down,
won't you?'

'Yes, but the night staff will look after you, and
I'm here again in the morning. You'll be all right.'
She gave him an encouraging smile before going
back to the office.

Paul had left the ward but Russell was still there,

sitting on the edge of the desk, telephoning.
finished speaking and slammed the receiver do
as she appeared, fixing her with a searching st
when she sat down to do her writing.

'Are you serious about Waring?' he deman
brusquely.

She swallowed back her rising resentment, de
mined not to be upset by his imperious mann
'Since you ask, no, but I don't see that it's any
your business.'

His eyes, meeting hers, sparked hostility. 'Lo
Russell,' she went on, laying down her pen a
making a great effort to keep calm, 'I know P
pretty well . . . he's been around for some time n
and I know I'm just the flavour of the month for
time being. Let's leave it at that, shall we?'

It was a mute appeal for a ceasefire, but
persisted in showing his disapproval. 'You seen
enjoy his attentions, anyway,' he snapped.

'And why shouldn't I enjoy a bit of harmless fi
Heaven knows we can do with some light relie
this job. In any case, Paul's kisses are a darned si
less objectionable than some I could mention,'
flared out of sheer pique.

'You make that perfectly clear. Better watch
or you'll land in trouble again,' and he stalked av
in a huff.

Gina's stomach was churning. She could h
wept with vexation. No matter how hard she trie
seemed impossible not to quarrel with the man.
how dare he speak to her like that! He had ov
stepped the mark this time. Apart from work,
decided to have nothing more to do with him.

The few remaining days to Christmas whittled away. There was much to be done both on and off duty. On her last day off Gina went up to the West End to complete her shopping, buying presents for the staff of Harvey Ward and family presents to take with her when she went to Melly's for the New Year.

She had arranged to meet her father for a meal in the evening and she found him in an optimistic frame of mind.

'So you enjoyed your weekend at Lyndhurst, did you?' she enquired when they were settled in the smart Italian restaurant he took her to.

'Yes . . . not that anyone took too much notice of me,' he smiled. 'The baby was the centre of attention. Nice little fellow, though. I'll be going down again for the holiday. What do you think I should take him?'

'Something for his bank account I should think,' Gina suggested. 'He's got plenty of everything for the moment.'

They studied the menu and gave their order, and while waiting to be served Mr Brent produced a small jewellery box from his pocket. 'I got these out East. Do you think your mother will like them?'

Opening the box Gina admired the small emerald earrings. 'Oh Dad, they're lovely. I'm sure she will. What—um—what about the future?'

'Well, I'm hoping Laura will be coming back to Kensington in January,' he said.

'I hope so, too,' put in Gina. 'Mum would never have let you go out wearing that tie with that shirt! Too many stripes!'

'So you prefer me when I'm henpecked, do you?' he teased.

'Let's face it, you need keeping in order. Like one or two other guys I know,' she added darkly.

He looked intrigued. 'Would one of those be Sir Richard Steele's son? I thought you two seemed to be getting on rather well the other night.'

She laughed. 'Don't let that fool you. We were just putting on a show for the parents. We're not exactly what you would call soul mates. Yes, he's one who often needs cutting down to size,' she agreed, 'although usually I'm the one who gets decimated in the end,' she concluded ruefully.

'Fine type of man, if he's anything like his father. Not always easy to get along with though, these dedicated people. Sir Richard told me that medicine has always been his son's driving force. He thinks of it to the exclusion of all else.'

'Not quite all else,' corrected Gina. 'He does have a sort of girlfriend.'

Her father smiled. 'He'd be a queer sort of bloke if he didn't . . . and he must have plenty of opportunities with his looks. There you are you see, parents don't always know their own children.'

'No,' she agreed. Russell's ruggedly handsome face rose in her mind. She had intimated to her father that she had no time for the man, and yet arrogant, maddening and unreasonable though he might be, there remained that subtle chemistry to melt her defences whenever they were together. Pure animal attraction, she tried to tell herself. When they ceased to see each other, as would be bound to happen one day, then she would cease to think about him. The trouble was, she couldn't help thinking about him. She loved thinking about him. It was a kind of delicious torment she put herself through. Unfortunately it was a futile exercise since it led nowhere.

'Oh, Gina,' her father said, 'I've just remembered, your mother gave me a box of Christmas goodies to bring back for you. You came up on the train, did you? You'd better come back to the flat with me to pick them up and I'll run you home afterwards.'

By the time they had eaten and gone back to Kensington it was after eleven before Gina arrived back at her own flat with her shopping and the hamper. Snow had started to fall in earnest, large feathery flakes drifting in the light of the street lamps but melting when they hit the pavement. Some settled on her bright hair as she ran the short distance to the front porch after waving goodbye to her father.

Esther was still up and the living room table deep in wrapping papers and ribbons. She greeted her flatmate merrily as Gina dumped her packages on the settee, shaking the moisture from her hair. 'Hi! Have a good day?'

'Great. I'll show you what I've bought in a minute. D'you want some coffee?'

'Please,' nodded Esther. 'There was a phone call for you earlier,' she added, 'Russell Steele.'

Gina paused in the act of stripping off her coat on the way to the kitchen. 'Russell . . . what did he want?'

'He didn't say. I asked did he want you to call him

back, but he said it wasn't important, he'll see you at work. Not tomorrow though, he's going to a one-day symposium on cytotoxic drugs or something.'

'Oh!' Frowning, Gina went on to make their drinks. What could he possibly have wanted? Maybe he realised he'd gone too far in criticising her conduct with Paul the other day. Maybe he wanted to apologise; except that he wasn't the apologising kind. Oh well, she would doubtless know soon enough.

Back in the sitting room she opened up the box her mother had sent and found a Christmas cake, mince pies, mixed nuts and raisins, and some home-made rum truffles. 'Ooh! My mother's speciality! You try one of these,' she said, offering the box to Esther.

The girls showed each other the gifts they had bought. Esther produced a double album of *The Lord of the Rings*. 'Look, I got this for Chris. He's potty about Tolkien.' She picked out a holly-strewn piece of paper and began to wrap the record with loving care.

Starting to parcel up some of her own presents, Gina found herself wondering what kind of record she might have chosen had she been buying one for Russell.

Her thoughts went back to the telephone call, and she indulged in a flight of fancy. Suppose, as a peace offering, he had been going to suggest taking her to another concert, since Fiona was away. Hardly likely. And in any case, she wouldn't want to be Fiona's stand-in.

Esther brought her down to earth. 'We put up our decorations in the ward today. When are you doing yours?'

'Tomorrow. That reminds me, I mustn't forget to take those Santa Claus cut-outs in. Good thing I got them when I did . . . I bought the last six.' On the other hand, it was more probable that he wanted to take her to task over something. She racked her brains trying to recall some sin of omission, but she could think of none.

CHAPTER NINE

HARVEY Ward had at last put on its party face. T
ward and the dayroom glittered with seasonal
corations. Mimi's little Christmas tree glowed
the centre table. Lynn had tied an enormous
satin bow around her large vase of holly. Sa
Claus in his spaceship zoomed between the b
and bare walls were ornamented with the patie
greetings cards. The staff were pleased with th
efforts and a generally lighthearted atmosph
prevailed.

They were less busy than usual, some of the m
mobile patients having been allowed home for
holiday. Meanwhile the nurses were making ev
effort to brighten the stay of those who still nee
to remain for treatment.

Although she was off at four-thirty on Christ
Eve, Gina did not hurry away; she lingered hav
a friendly chat with some of the patients. She
long since discovered that even the most awkw
or reticent of individuals would respond to
warmth of a genuine personal interest.

Talking with old Reuben Chambers she
delighted to hear that he'd had a visitor on her
off.

'It was a lady from the Young Wives' Club at
church,' he told her. 'That minister who cam
see me arranged it. Nice young woman. Told m

about her kids and what they've got them for their stockings. Lives not far from me and she's promised to come and see me when I go home. Don't know whether she meant it.'

'I expect she did, Mr Chambers. Those sort of people are usually sincere,' said Gina.

'Well, that's the impression I got. We seemed to hit it off. Anyway, I shall see her again tonight,' he went on cheerfully. 'They're coming round the wards singing carols and she said she'd look out for me.'

Gina at last left the hospital well satisfied with the state of things on her ward. There had been no sign of Russell. She didn't know whether to be glad or sorry about that and she was still in the dark as to the reason for his phone call. It couldn't have been important, she decided, since he hadn't bothered to follow it up. All the same it preyed on her mind, not knowing.

Back at the flat she found Esther ready to leave for home. 'Promise you will come over to us if you get fed up, won't you?'

'Okay, thanks, but I'll be all right,' Gina said. 'I quite like Christmas on the ward. Only routine work with a bit of luck. No medics getting under your feet wanting things done now if not sooner. And I'll have Lynn and Zoe and Mimi on with me . . . they're a great bunch. There'll be the usual rave-up in the doctors' mess, I'll probably go to that.'

In the process of getting out of her uniform dress she began to strip it of all the impedimenta—badges, watch, scissors, pens, pencil-torch. Digging into her hip pocket she drew a sharp breath as she pulled out a bunch of keys. 'Oh, help! Look what I've walked off with!'

'The ward keys?' Esther gave a short laugh and glanced at her watch. 'Not to worry, you can still get them back in time for the next drugs round. Get changed and I'll give them a ring to say you're on your way, just in case they're looking for them.'

'Thanks.' Gina hurried to her room, put on her jeans and a sweater, grabbed her duffel coat and drove back to the hospital. Her cheeks were glowing from the frosty air, her eyes starry as she hurried up to the ward and handed over the keys to Zoe. 'Sorry about that. Hope it didn't put you on the spot.'

'No, we hadn't even missed them until your friend rang.'

Gina wiped imaginary sweat from her brow. 'Saved again!' It would have been just her luck, she thought, to have had Russell show up and want something they couldn't get at. With a sigh of relief she made for the lift to take her back down to the ground floor. When it arrived from the floor above the doors slid open to reveal Paul Waring with Peter Smythe, and leaning against the wall behind them was Russell.

'Hi!' Paul greeted her, holding his arms wide in welcome. 'Just what I ordered for my stocking!'

'Optimist!' returned Gina with a good-natured grin.

'Never gives up, does he?' joked Peter. 'Give him "E" for effort anyway.'

Russell said nothing, but she sensed the chill in the air as Paul put his arm around her shoulders. 'Take no notice of him, baby. Sour grapes. We're just going for a quickie in the mess,' he added as they reached the ground floor. 'Come and get filled with the Christmas spirit.'

She hesitated. Esther would have gone on home by now so she might as well enjoy some company as spend a lonely evening. Russell also might unbend enough to tell her why he had phoned, but she was not going to ask. 'Okay,' she agreed, and they walked along together gossiping.

The messroom also was festooned with paper garlands and balloons and there was a goodly sprinkling of off-duty staff relaxing after the day's exertions. Paul stuck a paper crown on Gina's windblown curls and kissed her on the nose. 'What will you have?'

'Just a coke, please. And I'll open the can myself, if you don't mind.'

'You don't trust me?' he declared indignantly.

'Not any further than I can see you.'

He tutted, shook his head in mock reproof and went off to collect the drinks for them all.

'So you've learned sense at last, have you?' put in Russell, his seeking eyes making her feel utterly defenceless.

Her colour came and went. She half-laughed. 'I don't get caught out twice like that.'

'Famous last words?' he returned with a cynical curl of his lips.

Gina bridled. 'I'll let you know when I need a nanny!'

'Well, you need something. Maybe another ru
awakening!'

Peter looked mystified. 'Are you two startin;
double act?'

'What's this about a double act? What an
missing?' demanded Paul, returning with th
drinks.

Gina smiled but said nothing as she pulled
cap off her coke can and soon afterwards Russ
excused himself and went over to talk with so
others.

In spite of the festive atmosphere Gina's spi
zeroed. She made an effort to join in the frivol
banter of her companions, but her eyes k
straying in the direction of the registrar who sto
in amiable conversation with some of the thea
staff. On one occasion he met her gaze and
quickly looked away, wretched at his frigid
pression.

She told herself what an idiot she was, letting
obsession with the man get the better of her. V
should she let him upset her? She was going to fi
it; there were plenty of other people who found
company enjoyable. To prove her point she
about entering wholeheartedly into the so
mood and attracted more than her fair share
attention from various housemen.

Someone put on a tape and Paul claimed her f
smoochy dance. 'Too bad we can't paint the to
red tonight,' he murmured, his moustache tickl
her ear. 'I've got to shoot down to Suffolk for
family celebrations, or the old lady will never f
give me. Come with me?'

Gina smiled, knowing it wasn't a serious invitation. 'You'd have a shock if I said yes; actually I'm working tomorrow.'

'Too bad. We'll have to get together in the New Year.' He went on to talk of his family and of his father who was a vicar and she began to understand a little his rebellion against a rather strict upbringing. But he was much nicer when he was being serious.

Even so, Gina was still acutely conscious of Russell's presence in the room. Just by being there he seemed to rob her of her power to concentrate on anyone else. He continued to keep his distance, but she felt that he had her under observation; that nothing she said or did escaped his notice. It was most disquieting and after a while she made her excuses and left.

Footsteps followed her down the corridor as she went in the direction of the car park. Instinctively, without turning, she knew who it was. She reached the swingdoors and a tremor went through her as a hand came over her shoulder to push open the door. She knew his own special aura, that mixture of masculine warmth and the pleasant tang of his skin.

'Thank you,' she said, turning on the forecourt and looking up into Russell's face as she pulled up the hood of her duffel coat. Sleet had begun to come on the wind and she shivered after the warmth of the hospital.

'Off home now?' he asked, solemn-faced but with no sign of his earlier rancour.

She nodded. He walked along beside her towards the parked cars, putting a steadying hand on her elbow when she almost slipped on an icy patch. Reaching her car, she found ice glazing the windscreen.

'You'll need a scraper. Have you got one?' he asked.

'Yes.' She unlocked the door and reached inside the pocket for the scraper and her can of antifreeze. Shaking the tin, she threw it back with an expression of annoyance. 'Blow! That's empty.'

She wondered if he would criticise her for that, but he merely said: 'I'll get mine,' and made for his own car. Coming back with his aerosol he took the scraper out of her hand and set about clearing the windscreen and windows.

'That's fine,' she murmured, 'Thanks.'

He stayed to close the door when she got in and waited while she started the engine and fastened her seat belt. 'Mind how you go . . . there'll be black ice about.'

'Bye!' She flashed him a shy smile and drove away in a state of utter bewilderment. His own expression as he'd watched her go was a curious mixture of concern and something else.

He had her completely baffled. One moment he was being so beastly to her she could have exploded with righteous indignation; the next moment there he was treating her like a queen, behaving as though nothing was too much trouble. Why couldn't he always be sweet and reasonable?

Don't be a fool! she upbraided herself. Russell wasn't singling her out for any special attention tonight. He would have done as much for anyone else in need of help, so she had better not start reading anything into that. And maybe it was just as well that he wasn't always charming to her. It would only encourage her stupid preoccupation with him.

Reaching home without too much difficulty, she let herself into the empty house and switched on all the lights for company. She wondered if he, too, would be going home to an empty house that night, unless he were sleeping at the hospital. Perhaps he'd be ringing Fiona in Gstaad; Fiona, the girl who belonged to the world of class and privilege. Did Fiona appreciate how lucky she was to have the affection of a man like Russell? Because although he could be irritating and overbearing he also had many sterling qualities. He had integrity, foresight and inspiration where work was concerned. Coupled with which there was that devastating charm he could exercise whenever he chose.

Gina knew that with only the slightest en- couragement she would have little power to resist him. When he wasn't being impossible she had to admit to finding him endearing. And he excited her senses in a way that no other man had ever done. She sighed heavily and resolved yet again not to indulge herself by thinking about him.

After making herself some coffee she switched on the television and put her feet up on the settee. There was a lighthearted Christmas show on which helped to divert her thoughts. Some fifteen minutes later the telephone rang and she went out into the hall to answer it.

'Is that you, Gina?'

She recognised the voice at once and her heart skipped a beat. 'Yes?' she said.

'Oh, so you did get home all right. Thought I'd better check.'

There was a smile in her voice as she answered: 'It's Russell, isn't it? Yes, I made it, all in one piece.'

'Good. Now I shall be able to sleep soundly. What are you doing?'

'Well, I was sitting in front of the box, having a cup of coffee.'

'On your own?'

'Yes.' It did not occur to her to pretend otherwise. 'What are *you* doing?'

'I'm in a similar situation . . . and kicking myself at this moment.'

'Oh? Why's that?'

'Missed my cue tonight. Something I don't often do. I'll tell you about it when I see you.'

They chatted on amicably for a few moments until at last he said: 'Well, goodnight, Gina. Sleep well.'

Fat chance! she thought as she put down the phone and went back to the living room, finding it impossible after that to concentrate on the programme. She relived their conversation again and again. *Stop being nice to me Russell . . . I can't bear it!* she agonised.

On Christmas morning the family phoned her. She spoke to them all—Melly and John, her father and mother.

The bird had been in since eight o'clock, her

mother said, and they were just about to open their presents. 'There are some things for you here, love, things we couldn't post. I'll get Dad to bring them up when he comes. We're missing you. Have a nice day and don't work too hard.'

Afterwards, feeling nostalgic picturing them all together, Gina lay in the bath wallowing in the scent of some new bath oil. She daydreamed about Christmasses past, remembering the excitement of unpacking her stocking as a child; the fascination of little things like squeaky blowers, chocolate coins, pocket-sized dolls and the miniature china animals she had loved to collect.

It was only natural that the magic should fade as you left childhood behind. She supposed you lived it again through the next generation. Those days were still to come for Melly's baby. If she never had a child of her own she would have to settle for being an indulgent aunt, Gina thought wistfully.

Dismissing sentimental memories, she dressed with care in a fresh blue uniform and polished up the silver buckle on her belt. With the hospital party in mind she packed an uncrushable dress to change into that evening, together with shoes and accessories, and set off for the special lunch in the sisters' dining room. It was a much merrier gathering than usual. Gina found even some of the more formal nursing officers becoming positively friendly over a glass of sherry.

At one o'clock with a feeling of well-being she arrived to take the report on Harvey Ward. She found the patients relaxed and comfortable, enjoying the leisurely atmosphere and looking forward to their visitors. All the staff, herself included, sported tinsel trimming around the edge of their caps and necessary treatments were carried out with the minimum of fuss.

There had been crackers to accompany the patients' lunch of turkey and Christmas pudding. Going round the ward Gina noticed that Reuben's was still intact on his locker. 'Saving your cracker, Mr Chambers?' she smiled, pausing by his bed.

His pale blue eyes twinkled. 'Yes, Sister, I was waiting for you.'

She laughed and pulled it with him. They read the motto and she set the paper crown on his white hair, glad to find him cheerful. He looked very different from the neglected and under-nourished old man they had admitted. 'Did you enjoy the carols last night?'

'Yes, they were grand. Reckon this is the best Christmas I've had for a long time. Funny thing to say, isn't it, when you're in hospital?'

'Shhh!' she whispered, putting her fingers to her lips, 'Keep it under your hat or they'll all be wanting to come in.'

With the arrival of visitors the nurses were able to take a breather. They gathered together in the office, talking and dipping into more sweets that had come their way. Everything was well ahead and Gina decided to let the first shift go off early. 'No panic anywhere. We'll be able to cope.'

The remaining staff easily managed the few calls on their services and Gina herself took round the afternoon teas. She noticed that Mrs Colby, sitting at the far end of the ward with her husband, seemed somewhat downcast. 'Did you have a problem getting here?' she asked, knowing there was a limited bus service.

'No, I've got the car outside,' returned Mrs Colby. 'I'm a bit tired, that's all. It's been a hectic few days. I've got all my family coming over to-morrow.'

'Been overdoing it, she has,' her husband put in with a meaning glance at Gina. 'I wish you'd tell her she ought to take a bit more care of herself, Sister. I mean, what am I going to do if she cracks up, eh?'

'Well, let's hope we shan't need to keep you in too much longer, Mr Colby. Then it'll be your turn to look after her.'

The woman herself shrugged with exaggerated tolerance. 'He's an old fusspot. Take no notice of him.'

She seemed disinclined to say any more and so Gina gave Mr Colby an equivocal smile and went on her way. Returning to the office she began to make a start on some essential paperwork before the evening round of activity.

Lynn Davis looked in to report that one of the patients was complaining of a headache. She had brought his medication sheet and Gina glanced through it. 'Probably too much excitement. Give him a couple of Paracetamol for now and see if that helps.'

She glanced at her watch as the visitors began to drift out. Some paused for a quick word and others gave her a cheery wave before going back to their own homes. Mrs Colby was amongst the last to leave. Looking up from her writing Gina noticed

her pause on her way down the ward, catching onto
someone's bedrail for a moment as though breathless. Recovering, Mrs Colby set off again, holding
an arm across her ample figure, but as she passed
the office door she caught her bottom lip between
her teeth.

The woman was clearly in some distress. Gina
jumped up and went after her, laying a hand on her
arm as she left the main ward. 'Mrs Colby, what's
the matter?'

Breathing heavily, the woman paused. There
were beads of perspiration on her pink face and a
kind of panic in her eyes. 'Oh Sister, I do feel
terrible,' she confessed with a quick glance back
towards the ward, 'but I don't want my Henry to
know.'

'You come in here for a minute.' Gina led her
into an empty sideward and sat her down on a chair.
'He won't see you from here. Now, what exactly
is wrong. Have you got a pain anywhere in
particular?'

'Yes, it's been griping me off and on ever since I
got up this morning, and since I've been here it's
got that bad, I don't know how I sat through the
visiting. Oh Lord!' Her face screwed up and she
bent forward, both arms hugging her abdomen. In
a few moments the spasm appeared to pass. With a
groan of relief she gradually straightened up.

'You haven't been feeling too well for some time,
have you?' prompted Gina with a look of concern.

'No, not really. I've had a terrible lot of indigestion and heartburn. And I feel I've got something
pushing up against me here.' She rubbed a hand

loosely over her diaphragm. 'What do you think it is?' she appealed, her forehead creased with worry.

Gina raised her eyebrows noncommittally. 'That's difficult to say without an examination. It might be something quite simple, but I do think you ought to have a check-up. Why don't you call in at our Casualty Department, since you're here? Anyway, sit there for a minute. Would you like some water?'

'Yes, please. Ooh!' Mrs Colby's face began to tense again. 'Oh, my God!' she muttered, and a prolonged guttural groan came from her throat as she clutched at her belly.

Gina frowned as a startling possibility dawned on her. She saw there might be need for urgency and darting outside, she grabbed Mimi Tong who was returning from her tea break. 'Mrs Colby's not well. I don't think she'd make it to Casualty. I'm going to try and find a doctor. Stay with her . . . get her coat off and get her onto the bed when she feels able.'

'Yes, Sister.' Mimi's kindly young face was all solicitude as she went to Mrs Colby's aid.

Zoe Wynford, also returning from her break, came from the main corridor. On her way to the phone, Gina paused to tell her staff nurse the problem. 'I suppose you haven't seen a houseman anywhere? I think she could be in labour.'

'*Mrs Colby?*' said Zoe, sounding incredulous. 'Well, Dr Steele was coming this way,' she added.

The swingdoor pushed open and Gina breathed a sigh of relief to see Russell strolling towards them, grey-suited and elegant. 'Oh! Am I glad to see you!' she said.

'That's encouraging at any rate,' he returned with a one-sided smile. 'What's the trouble?'

Quickly she explained the situation, adding her own suspicion. 'Her husband thinks she's convinced she's got a tumour, but she hasn't had medical advice. *I* wouldn't mind betting she's pregnant. Will you look at her? She feels very poorly.'

He agreed. 'Where is she?'

'In there,' said Gina, and after asking Zoe to take charge of the ward, she followed him into the sideroom.

Mimi had drawn the curtains across the windows and Mrs Colby now lay huddled up on the bed.

'Hallo, my dear,' Russell said quietly, his observant eyes taking note of her general condition. 'Sister thinks I should take a look at you. What seems to be the matter?'

'I don't know,' said Mrs Colby, very frightened. 'I think I'm going to die.'

'You look far too hale and hearty to be on the way out just yet,' said the doctor confidently. He laid his fingers on her pulse. 'That seems to be fine. Where's the pain?'

'All over, when it comes . . . and it goes right through to my back. It's excruciating.'

'Will you lie flat for me? And can we have her dress up please?' Russell murmured to Gina.

She lifted back Mrs Colby's jersey skirt. Her tights and pants sat below the swollen dome of her belly. Gina had seen that shape a good many times in the course of her nursing experience and she exchanged a significant glance with Russell.

'When was your last period, Mrs Colby?' he asked, his fingers gently probing the mass.

'Oh, ages ago. Is that when things start to go wrong, at the change?'

'No, it's a perfectly natural event. May I borrow your stethoscope, Gina?'

She handed him the instrument from her pocket and he listened carefully at various positions on the swelling. 'I'd better do an internal,' he decided, straightening up.

'Oh, I don't want to die,' she whimpered as another pain gripped her.

Gina hurried to fetch gloves and a lubricant while Russell took off his jacket, rolled up the sleeves of his crisp blue shirt and scrubbed his hands. When Mrs Colby's bout of pain had subsided his sensitive fingers made their exploration. His dark eyes, meeting Gina's, confirmed her views. 'Fully dilated,' he murmured.

'Well, Mrs Colby,' he went on, smiling at the woman, 'You've got something in there all right, but it's nothing to worry about. You're going to have a baby. Didn't you have any idea?'

Her mouth dropped open. '*Me?* A—a—baby? I *can't* be. I'm forty-six . . . we tried for years . . .'

'I can assure you that you are. Its heart is ticking away in there like billy'o.'

She was half-laughing, half-crying now. 'Dear God! You mean . . . these are labour pains?'

'That's right.' Russell looked across at Gina and grinned.

'Oh, that's incredible,' the woman was saying. 'I never dreamed . . . how long will it be?'

'Pretty soon, I should think. We certainly can't risk sending you over to the Maternity block, that's half-a-mile away. We'll have to deliver you here.'

Mimi, goggle-eyed, seemed momentarily stunned. 'You get Mrs Colby into a gown,' Gina urged, 'and I'll rustle up some equipment. Perhaps they can send us a midwife.'

Hastily she set about gathering together on a dressings trolley the things that might possibly be required, including plastic aprons for them all. There was a buzz of excitement amongst the staff who were all, by now, aware of the crisis although carrying on in the ward with proper discretion.

Having made all the emergency preparations she could, Gina phoned across to Maternity in the hope of being able to secure a midwife with the conventional equipment.

'Looks like you'll have to make do with me and what we've got,' she had to report to Russell, pushing in her make-do delivery kit, 'They're rushed off their feet on Maternity at the moment.'

'Oh, I think we can manage it between us,' he said as she passed him an apron. 'We'll give her some pethidine, shall we?'

'Yes, I've got some here.' Gina broke the top of an ampoule and Russell drew up the drug and injected it into Mrs Colby's thigh. 'There you are, my dear. That will relax your muscles and make things a bit easier for you.'

'Now I know what's happening I can bear anything,' said the woman, still lost in amazement at what was happening to her. 'And I've got nothing ready . . . no clothes to put it in, poor little soul.'

Gina smiled, pouring some Savlon solution into a bowl. 'We'll find you some clothes, and once people know I expect you'll be showered with gifts.' She looked up to find Russell watching her with a curious expression in his eyes. She couldn't interpret it. She only knew that it made her feel happy; that for once there was no animosity between them.

The pains were good and strong now and Mrs Colby gasped and gritted her teeth and gripped Mimi's hand, stifling a cry. When the sharpness had subsided, Gina gently wiped the woman's hot sweaty face.

'That's fine,' Russell told her cheerfully. 'Another contraction like that last one and we're in business. Let me know when it's coming.'

She lay getting her breath back, puffing a little. 'Gosh! I hope the baby'll be all right. I haven't had any extra vitamins or anything . . .'

'You seem to me to be healthy enough,' Russell observed, sitting at the foot of the bed while they waited. 'D'you smoke?'

Mrs Colby shook her head. 'And I don't drink either.'

'And you haven't had any illnesses lately?' She shook her head again and began to grip the sides of the bed, her face screwing up in suspense. 'It's coming!' she gasped.

Russell was ready. 'Right . . . try to do what I tell you and it won't be long.'

She co-operated splendidly with all he asked of her, pushing and panting alternately, supported by the nurses, and presently without too much difficulty the head was born. A small dark head with a puce-coloured wrinkled little face. Quickly Gina passed cotton-wool swabs to the doctor, who cleaned the mucus from the tiny features. Another strong contraction followed and he was able to ease the shoulders through, after which the rest of the body slipped out easily. The infant let out a mewling wail after his first intake of breath.

'Mrs Colby, you've got a son,' said Russell with a broad smile.

The mother, lying back exhausted on her pillow, raised her head to look. 'Is he all right?' she asked anxiously.

Russell was deftly examining the new arrival. 'Yes, he's absolutely perfect. Five fingers on each hand . . . five toes apiece . . . and all his bits and pieces intact. You can hold him in a minute.'

Helping him deal with the cord, Gina felt oddly emotional. She didn't quite know why. It was all mixed up with the miracle of birth and their mutual involvement in it. She felt completely at one with him, and when he handed her the child there was a softness in his brown eyes that made her heart turn over.

Wrapping the infant in a cotton blanket, she laid it in Mrs Colby's arms, fighting the constriction in her throat. 'There you are. Isn't he gorgeous?'

'Oh! You're beautiful . . . beautiful!' the woman cooed over him, her face radiant.

The sideward seemed full of happiness. Mimi bit

a trembling lip, her eyes overbright. Gina averted her gaze, and found Russell's eyes still fixed upon her. He was suppressing a smile. 'Shall we deal with the placenta?' he suggested.

She went back to join him and while they checked that all was in order, Mrs Colby carried on hugging her baby. 'What will your daddy say?' she murmured.

They all looked at each other open-mouthed and Gina laughed. 'Daddy! I'd forgotten all about him. He's going to have a shock,' she said.

'A few more minutes won't make much difference,' decided Russell. 'We'll get her tidied up first . . . she's going to need a stitch there. Then he can come along and be introduced.'

'And you'd like some tea, I'm sure,' said Gina to the new mother. She despatched Mimi to make some for them all.

There was a tap on the door and a midwife bustled in with her sterile pack. 'Oh, am I too late?' she said. 'Sorry, it couldn't be helped. You managed then?'

Russell's straight eyebrows quirked humorously. 'Yes, the main feature went well. You can stay and help with the clearing up if you like so that Sister Brent can get back to her ward.'

'Yes, of course,' said the midwife, 'and we'll have to get her transferred as soon as we can. There is a bed.' She rolled up her sleeves and went over to inspect the baby to make sure that everything met with her approval.

'And perhaps you'll tell Mr Colby what's been going on, will you?' Russell's gaze met and held

Gina's for a moment, causing more havoc in her breast.

'I will, if you'd like me to.' She stripped off her apron and went to the sink to wash her hands, turning a warm smile in Mrs Colby's direction. 'Your tea won't be long, and we'll bring Dad along to see you both as soon as you're ready.'

CHAPTER TEN

FLEET of foot, Gina sped down the ward to prepare the unsuspecting father for the surprise of his life. 'It's a boy!' she whispered to Zoe and Lynn who were in the middle of the drugs round.

She found Mr Colby settling down to read a new paperback his wife had brought him. He put it down and looked at her enquiringly when she stopped beside him, bright-eyed and eager. 'Hallo, Sister,' he said, 'You look as if you've won the pools.'

'Well, I *feel* as if I have. But it's not me. You're the one who's hit the jackpot. I've got something of a shock for you.'

He stared at her blankly. 'Oh? What's that?'

'Mr Colby, your wife wasn't ill, I'm glad to say. But she *was* pregnant!' His mouth gaped as she paused to give him time to take it in. 'She gave birth in our sideward a few minutes ago. You've got a lovely little son.'

Astonishment, bewilderment, incredulity and delight passed across his face in rapid succession. 'Good God! So that's what the matter was?' He shook his head in wonder as he finally absorbed the truth. 'H—how is she? Did she have a bad time?'

'She's absolutely fine, and she did very well. You'd have thought she was used to having babies instead of this being her first. We haven't been able to weigh him yet because we don't have any baby scales, but I would guess he's about six pounds.'

'Well, I'm blowed! What a blessing she was here.' He bit trembling lips and suddenly caught her hand and kissed it. 'Thanks for looking after her, Sister. Cor! Would you believe it, me a dad! It's a bloody miracle! When do I get to see them?'

'Quite soon now,' smiled Gina. 'They're just giving her a wash and making her comfortable.'

Mr Morgan in the next bed had heard most of the conversation. 'What's that, Harry?' he wheezed, 'Your missus has just had a baby?'

Mr Colby nodded, beaming foolishly, and the other patient offered his congratulations. 'We all ought to get something stronger than cocoa tonight, eh Sister?'

A Christmas baby had just been born on Men's Medical! The news flashed round the ward like lightning and Mr Colby found himself the butt of much good-natured teasing and wisecracks. In a few moments they were joined by Russell who added his own compliments as he shook Mr Colby by the hand.

'Thanks Doctor. How are they both?'

'Your wife couldn't be better and your son is perfect,' Russell assured him.

'When can I see them? I shan't believe it till I do.'

'You can go along now. We're getting her transferred to Maternity as soon as possible, but you can stay with them until they go.'

'Thanks. Thanks both of you, for everything,' Mr Colby murmured gratefully, still scarcely able to credit what had overtaken him.

'Our pleasure, wasn't it, Sister,' returned Russell, exchanging a smile with Gina. 'It made a nice change from ulcers and bronchial problems.' He went off to write up the case notes to accompany mother and baby when they were collected from Harvey Ward.

Gina helped the excited father into his dressing-gown, found him his slippers, and took him along to meet his family. Mrs Colby, clad in a nightdress borrowed from one of the women's wards, lay in her freshly made bed, tired but elated. Her new son was alongside her, swaddled in his blanket and as yet still unwashed. The midwife was still fluttering around, doing this and that, but Gina left the parents together to rejoice in their good fortune. She had her own work now to catch up on.

Russell was still in the office, writing, but he had disappeared when Gina made her way to the sluice with a specimen for labelling. She found the midwife there, disposing of her rubbish. She was a middle-aged, rather talkative soul, and engaged Gina in a friendly conversation.

'The porter will be up soon. I thought I'd better wait around to carry the baby. I expect you've been held up long enough.'

'We didn't mind,' said Gina. 'We enjoyed it, as a matter of fact.'

'Have you done your midder?'

'No, but I did my stint on Obstetrics, and there were no complications with this one, thank goodness. Anyway, Dr Steele did the delivery.'

'He's super, isn't he,' enthused the midwife.

'Wish he was one of ours. I suppose you didn't do a urine test?' she prattled on.

'Heavens, no!' laughed Gina, 'We were only just about in time to deliver the baby.'

'Yes, of course. Ah well, we can do all that when we get her over the road.' She looked at her watch. 'Time that porter was here. I'll go and check with your student that she put all Mrs Colby's property in a bag. And she'll need to be well wrapped up . . . it's cold outside. Do you realise it's Christmas Day?' she flung over her shoulder on the way out, 'We've been so busy I'd almost forgotten.'

Gina hadn't forgotten. It wasn't every day they had a birth on Harvey Ward. The news had by now filtered round the hospital and a nursing officer looked in to ask if help was needed, but in reality Gina guessed she was just curious to see the new infant.

Countless other interruptions followed, so that what had started out as a fairly tranquil day was rapidly becoming anything but.

'Is that Harvey, or Maternity?' came Sal Yates' giggly voice over the telephone.

'Oh, so you've heard down there, have you?' said Gina.

'You can't keep all the excitement to yourself in this place.'

'Look, if you're all twiddling your thumbs in theatre,' Gina joked, 'we're still up to our eyes in it, so why not come up and give us a hand?'

'I've done my whack for today,' returned Sally. 'Just wanted to ask you if you're going to the party tonight?'

'Yes, if ever I get off I shall be.'

'Right, I'll let you get on. See you there.'

Just as they were about to serve suppers the porter at last arrived. Reluctantly Mr Colby kissed his wife goodbye and watched as they disappeared into the corridor, the mother tucked up on the trolley, the baby in the arms of the midwife.

'Come along back to bed now,' said Gina. 'You've had enough excitement for one day. We'll try and get you over to see them tomorrow. I'll bring the phone along for you after supper and you can get cracking and tell your friends the good news. Didn't your wife tell me she was expecting visitors tomorrow?'

'Yes, that's right. Her mum and her sisters. I shall have to get on to them or they'll wonder what's up. They're going to be staggered.'

She left him making a list of all the people he had to contact and all the arrangements they would now have to make. Going back to the office, Gina thought she had better make a start on her report for the night staff.

A drink that had been made for her was on the desk but now cold. She wrote for a while before picking up the mug and carrying it back to the kitchen to make fresh coffee before the evening round of activity. Although the rest of the staff had taken their tea break as usual Gina had not stopped since coming on at midday.

Now, pleasantly weary, she waited for the kettle to boil and gazed absently out of the fourth floor window. Lights of other wards winked across the darkness and a sprinkling of snow lightened ledges and rooftops.

What a wonderful Christmas present it had been for the Colbys, she mused. Miracles did sometimes happen. It had been something of a miracle, too, the way she had felt working with Russell. No matter how many times you saw a baby born each was a different, spellbinding experience. But this occasion had been special; touched with magic. And she had known instinctively that something had catalysed in there between herself and the doctor, although nothing had been said.

The heavy kitchen door creaked open and Russell's deep voice cut across her thoughts. 'A penny for them, Gina.

He closed the door and leaned against it, hands in trouser pockets, heart-stoppingly handsome, studying her with keen-eyed interest.

'I was thinking about this afternoon,' she said. 'I bet you didn't know what you were in for when you showed up.'

'No. My visit had quite a different motive.' A smile played around the corners of his mouth. 'It was personal, as a matter of fact.'

'Oh?' She waited for him to explain, but he simply carried on looking at her in a manner which sent her blood surging. The kettle boiled. She switched it off and reached for the coffee jar, drawing a deep breath. 'Would you like some?'

'Leave that and come over here,' he ordered. 'I have to talk to you.'

Her pulse rate doubled, pounding in her ears. Perversely she carried on with what she was doing.

It was a kind of desperate gesture of independence. 'Talk away. I'm not stopping you.'

'I said leave that and come here!' he repeated in a tone that compelled obedience.

She hesitated, put down the coffee jar and took a few steps towards him, her feet obeying against her will. 'Well,' she said lightly, stopping a yard in front of him, 'if you want to whisper in my shell-like ear, what's wrong with your own legs?'

'My legs are fine. But if I move away from this door someone is likely to come barging in, and I don't want to be disturbed.'

He put out a hand to pull her nearer. His touch sent an explosion of longing through her veins, but she met his vigilant eyes defiantly. 'What have I done?' she demanded.

'Why should you think you've done anything? It's more, what you are,' he returned quietly. 'I phoned the other night, but you were out. Did the message get through?'

'Yes, I wondered when you were going to mention it. Did you want to apologise for your insufferable cheek the last time you were up here?' she suggested flippantly.

A trace of amusement flickered across his face. 'No, I didn't. I meant every word I said. But I thought it was high time we came to some kind of understanding, and I thought if we met over a civilised meal it might help.'

'Oh! Is that all?'

'Yes . . . and no. The next time I saw you, you were *still* clowning around with Paul Waring, and I didn't feel at all civilised about it. Which made me do some very serious thinking.' The bleep in his pocket sounded and he groaned with annoyance. 'Damnation! This is hopeless.'

Letting go her hand, he made rapid strides for the ward phone, leaving her completely in the dark and her innards fluttery. What on earth was he driving at? And why should it incense him whenever she talked to Paul? It was stupid. She would have to put him straight about Paul because there really was no harm in him. He was more like an overgrown adolescent.

She was thinking out a tactful way to put this when Russell looked in again. 'I'll have to go. They want me on Casualty. Have you any plans for tonight?'

'Only the get-together in the mess.'

'Right. If I'm not back before you go I'll see you there, okay?'

'Yes . . . if you like . . .'

He was gone before she had got the words out, leaving her with her brain in a whirl. She went back to her coffee-making, trying to make sense of his remarks. *It's more what you are*, he'd said. What did he think she was? Not that he'd said it in a derogatory manner. In fact he had sounded, well, almost approving? She gave up trying to work it out and went back to the office to get on with her report.

Mimi and Lynn trundled past with the supper trolley now stacked with empty plates. They would then be starting on the four-hourlies and blood pressure readings and giving out washing bowls to those patients who could not get to the bathroom.

After that it would be beds and pressure areas. There were just four staff on that evening.

'I'll be with you soon,' Gina called to Lynn. 'I'll take one side of the ward with Mimi and you and Zoe can do the other.'

Finishing her clerking, she rolled up her sleeves and joined Mimi who had started to wash a helpless stroke patient. He could understand, although he could not talk, and they entertained him with an account of the excitement in the ward that afternoon. 'And let's hope that's our only Christmas bonus,' Gina smiled. 'We've just about caught up with ourselves now.' They smoothed his bottom sheet and changed his position before remaking the bed and passing on to the next patient.

But fate had not finished with Harvey Ward. Lynn came trotting over from seeing to Mr Morgan, who had an intravenous infusion in his arm. 'His bandage is soaking . . . Zoe thinks the drip must be blocked.'

Gina clapped a hand to her head. 'Oh, no! All right, you help Mimi here and I'll come and see.'

Zoe was unwinding the wet bandage from Mr Morgan's forearm.

'Sorry, Sister,' he said, 'I only just noticed it was like this.'

'It's not your fault, love. It happens,' returned Gina. She inspected the inflamed site of the needle. The infusion was escaping into the tissues instead of running into the vein. 'That'll need resiting. Shall we leave it for the night staff?' She looked at her watch. It was getting on for eight o'clock. 'Oh, better not. I'll ring for a houseman.'

Making for the phone, Gina walked straight into a whitecoated doctor, but he was a stranger to her.

'Good evening, Sister, everything all right here?' he enquired cheerfully.

He was a stockily built man with wiry brown hair cut fairly short. There were the usual accoutrements in his pockets and a name-badge on his lapel. *Thomas Flynn* her eyes took in as she spoke to him.

'Hallo, I haven't seen you before. Are you new here?'

'Yes, I'm a locum they've called in for the holiday.'

'Oh, I see. Well, as a matter of fact, you can help. One of our i.v. drips has tissued. Will you come and see to it?'

'Certainly.' He strolled along with her to take a look at the arm. 'Yes, I'll do that for you, if you'll get me the necessary.'

He seemed efficient enough, and very meticulous, washing his hands thoroughly before starting. 'What brand is this?' he asked as she stripped the covering off a fresh appliance.

'It's a Venflon. We find them very useful.'

'I've not dealt with that type before. I've been abroad for a couple of years. But you can show me how it goes. We'd better use the other arm, don't you think?'

She agreed and he searched out a suitable vein, cleansing the site with a steri-square before inserting the fresh cannula.

With Gina's expert guidance the job was completed without any trouble and the drip functioned well again. He seemed inordinately pleased with

himself at performing this relatively simple pro-
cedure. 'Thank you, Sister. I'm a bit out of touch
with things over here.'

'Thank *you*,' she said, walking with him towards
the door. 'I thought I was going to have trouble
finding someone.'

'Anything else I can do for you? Any pain-killers
you want written up?'

'No, we're all right so far. The night staff will get
in touch if they need anything. Do you want some
coffee?' she asked.

He hesitated, and as the telephone started to ring
she thought he seemed slightly nervous. 'No, I'd
better get on . . . mustn't hold you up,' and with a
charming smile he left her.

Going to the phone she felt there was something
odd about him, but dismissed it as shyness, being in
a strange environment. The caller was a talkative
relative of the Colbys wanting her good wishes
passed on. After delivering the message Gina went
back to Zoe to help finish the beds. 'Funny guy,
wasn't he?' she said.

It was some fifteen minutes later that Russell
Steele blew into the ward accompanied by two
stalwart men in trench coats. 'These gentlemen are
detectives,' he told her. 'Have you had a strange
houseman visit you?'

'Yes, actually we have, about fifteen minutes
ago.' Gina looked apprehensive. 'Why? Is anything
wrong?'

'We think he's an impostor. The office have been
ringing around trying to warn people, but your
phone was busy.'

'Oh dear!' she frowned. 'He just resited Mr Morgan's i.v.i. for us. He said he was a locum. His name was Thomas Flynn.'

'Been using a different handle everywhere, love,' put in one of the detectives.

'He seemed genuine . . . capable.'

'Yeah! That's what they all say. He's been working all the London hospitals this week, but he's bogus all right. Been a medical orderly probably, or maybe a failed student,' the detective went on. 'He knows the routine. Got away with some drugs in a couple of places. Did he ask you for any?'

'Well, no,' said Gina, 'but he did mention drugs.' Instinctively she felt in her pocket, making sure that the keys were safely there. She remembered the time she had needed to reprimand Sharon Evans for leaving the drugs trolley unattended; she hadn't liked doing so, but it had been a necessary warning.

'If he should come back try to keep him here and give us a buzz. Better check that your handbags are safe,' warned the detective.

'We keep them in a locked cupboard,' she said.

Russell decided he ought to check the man's handiwork and went back with her to see Mr Morgan's drip. 'Yes, that's fine,' he pronounced, and as they walked away, 'The fellow obviously has some practical experience, although I suppose he couldn't go wrong with you here. I'll see you later,' he reminded her.

At nine o'clock the night staff came on but it was nearer ten before Gina could get away. In the staff room she washed and changed, putting on her flattering black voile dress with its multi-coloured sparkling threads. A simple gold chain around her throat, gold earrings, high-heeled black patent sandals, and she cast off her exacting role as sister to become a private individual for the remainder of Christmas Day.

The trouble was, it was very difficult to divorce her two persona when all her thoughts were now centred upon a dark-haired, dark-eyed doctor who was soon to commandeer her for some reason of his own. She hoped he would not be too long in getting to the party, because it was intolerable being kept in suspense.

Tales of the bogus doctor were circulating in the mess when she arrived. Apparently he had visited a number of wards and fooled the people in charge, but he had finally been caught up with stealing money from a nurse's bag left lying around on Anderson Ward.

'They say it was Russell who first suspected that he wasn't what he made out to be and got in touch with the law,' Sally told Gina. 'Bright boy, that one.'

When Russell at last arrived and sought her out, the taped music and general merriment made private discourse virtually impossible.

'This isn't the right place for what I have to say. Let's find somewhere more private.' Taking her by the hand, he drew her in the direction of the door.

'All this cloak and dagger stuff, Russell,' she said with a slight laugh, 'What's the big mystery?'

He pulled her along the corridor towards the

deserted lecture room. Opening the door, he pushed her inside and shut it firmly behind them, jerking his head in the direction of the bony skeleton suspended from a stand. 'This'll do. *He* won't interrupt.'

Smiling nervously, Gina propped herself against one of the desks, gazing up at him with wide blue eyes. She felt her legs might let her down without support.

'Where did we get to?' he began, his nearness throwing her into a state of panic. Scarcely a foot between them. So near, and yet so far. Oh, how she wished his arms were about her instead of being thrust into his pockets.

'Y—you'd been doing some heavy thinking, you said. And please, if it's about Paul, let it drop. He's quite harmless. In fact when you know him better you'll find he's a decent sort, when he stops clowning.' The words came tumbling out of her. 'Anyway, it's hardly your place to . . .'

'Let's leave him out of this discussion.' Russell pushed a hand impatiently through his thick, dark hair. 'I'm not interested in talking about Waring. It's you and me and our volcanic reactions I'm concerned with.' He paused, his eyes searching her troubled face. 'When I phoned that night I told myself it was my intention to sort you out once and for all. I know now that it was really an excuse for getting to see you. When I *did* see you again, there you were with that . . . that blockhead . . .' He flagged her down with his hand as she opened her mouth to protest. 'I know, I know, he's got his good points, but that doesn't alter the fact that I wanted to throttle him with my bare hands. Now what do you think that means?'

'I don't know.' She shrugged, striving to appear in control although she was becoming more and more agitated. 'That you have an ungovernable temper, perhaps?'

'You're being deliberately thick, aren't you?' he accused, closing the gap between them and glaring down at her. 'Weighing up the symptoms, I came to the only possible diagnosis.'

'All right, so I'm thick. What symptoms?' she glared back, feeling as though her own limbs were as disjointed as the skeleton's.

His mouth began to twitch. 'Don't get stroppy with me, girl.' He put a hand on either side of her waist and raised her to her feet. 'I came to the conclusion that we are both victims of a serious cardiac condition. Brought about by a denial of basic needs.'

Her colour rose and her mouth went dry as her startled eyes gazed up at him and read the message in his ardent face. His hands, warm on her body, kept her knees from buckling. She swallowed. 'Wh—what are you on about? Say all that in plain English.'

'In plain English, my adorable, dotty Gina, it means that I'm mad about you. And although it may sound presumptuous, I would guess that you aren't entirely unaffected either. Come on, admit it.' He gave her a little shake, earnestly watching her bemused expression.

Was he actually saying that he loved her? 'I—I—' she gasped, her senses reeling. There had to be a catch. It was too marvellous to be true. And then a thought came to her. 'You're on the rebound from Fiona!' she accused fiercely.

He caught her to him, chuckling softly. 'My darling, my darling, so you were jealous too, were you? The classic symptom! I was wild with jealousy. I could have torn from limb to limb anyone who touched you.' He pressed a finger to the tip of her nose. 'No, I'm not on the rebound from Fiona. She's my mother's god-daughter. I'm a sort of big brother to her. I'm convenient to have around.'

A wide and incredulous smile spread over Gina's face. 'Oh! A bit like Mark and me, you mean?'

He drew her, unresisting, into the circle of his arms, claiming her willing mouth with his own, passionate and possessive. Her body seemed to fuse with his in the intensity of their love. It was almost too sweet to bear, this fulfilment of their longing.

Presently his hands cupped the curve of her head, his fingers running through her red-gold curls as he smothered her face and neck with kisses. 'What have you done to me?' he murmured. 'I've always been able to keep my private life in its proper place before. I certainly didn't intend getting serious with anyone until I'd at least got a consultancy under my belt. But when a pert-nosed redhead started coming between me and my studies, what else could I do?'

'You could have tried being nice to me sooner,' she returned, clasping her arms tightly around his neck. 'I respond to kindness.'

'A fat lot of encouragement you gave me. You were about the only woman I couldn't get through to. It took me a while to work out why we were always fighting. Defence mechanism on both our parts.'

Laughing softly, Gina reached up to kiss him again. 'I really did try hard to hate you. You were a swine to me most of the time.'

'You know why now. I was afraid of getting involved. But if guys like Waring don't keep their filthy mitts of you, I shall be a swine again.' He eyed her impishly. 'Do you know what I was thinking when we delivered Mrs Colby's baby?'

'The same as me, perhaps? That we were getting on the right wavelength at last?'

He shook his head. 'I went much further. I found myself wanting to get *you* with child.'

'Russell! That sounds like an improper suggestion,' she grinned.

'Quite the reverse. It means you're going to marry me as soon as we can arrange it.' He took off the gold signet ring from his little finger and slipped it onto Gina's ring finger. 'Will this do, until we can shop for the real thing? Just to remind you who you belong to.'

Voices and footsteps outside the door made them draw apart. It opened and another couple looked in, searching for seclusion. 'Oh, sorry,' they said with apologetic smiles.

'Come in, come in,' Russell invited, 'We're just leaving.'

Taking Gina's hand, he led her past them out of the room, closing the door behind him. She paused outside, fingering the heavy gold ring on her third finger and looking up at him, her face radiant. 'It's rather loose . . . I shouldn't like to lose it.'

He pushed it onto her middle finger and sealed it there with a kiss. 'Stop complaining. Now you probably won't be able to get it off. That'll set the tongues wagging, won't it?'

She smiled shyly. 'What are we going to do now? I don't think I want to go back to the party.'

'I knew we were kindred spirits.'

'Mince pies at my place? My mother sent me some.'

'Mince pies . . . and you?' he breathed, his eyes teasing. 'Is that the latest line in come-ons? I can hardly wait.'

'Have you got a better idea?'

He drew her once more into his fiercely enfolding arms. 'I did tell you I was an opportunist, didn't I?'

'You did,' she returned with reckless abandon.

His embrace tightened. 'I love you, darling,' he murmured huskily, and oblivious of passersby, their lips met again in mutual ecstasy.

Doctor Nurse Romances

Amongst the intense emotional pressures of modern medical life, doctors and nurses often find romance. Read about their lives and loves in the other three Doctor Nurse titles available this month.

SURGEON'S CHOICE
by Hazel Fisher

Cherry Mills takes the job as Senior Staff Nurse on the Gynae ward at St Monica's so that she can be near Scott Nicholson. But what chance has her love for the handsome consultant when it seems that both Sister Vinton and her cousin Margot have prior claims on him?

NURSE AT TWIN VALLEYS
by Lilian Darcy

Love on the rebound is definitely not for Nurse Orana Bowe. She has come to work at the Australian ski resort of Twin Valleys to escape from a broken heart, so she is determined not to fall for the first man she meets just because he resembles Dr Jack de Salis . . .

THE END OF THE RAINBOW
by Betty Neels

As a grateful niece, Olympia feels bound to work in her aunt's nursing home, though her life is little more than that of a dogsbody. Then fate takes a hand in the form of Dr Waldo van der Graaf . . .

Mills & Boon

the rose of romance